RIGHT CO

Lucy Wells

RIGHT COMMONERS

Right Commoners

Copyright ©Lucy Wells 2025

ISBN 978-1-326-40686-8

This is a work of fiction and any resemblance to people living or dead is entirely coincidental.

Dedicated

to

A return to abundance

health and prosperity

"This earth divided we will make whole so it will be a common treasury for all."

Leon Rosselson

Chapter one

It is autumn, the air is crisp. The perfectly still morning lacks any drying wind, but she pegs out the washing anyway.

Of the very many differing shades, the blue of this day is vivid cerulean such as a Madonna might choose for her best veil. And stitched upon it are a few fluffy clouds hanging peaceably by.

Scattering across the sky the short blue wavelengths beam calm and perhaps hope if it's needed in the vast heavens.

The crunch of gravel and a car stops in a passing place on the lane below the garden, the boom of a sound system is punched silent. The door clunks open, a couple of footsteps and then the release of a boot catch, and the hissing hydraulic rods release the tailgate. A couple of pigeons flap flirting on a telephone wire above.

This is the place they have chosen for the handover. A hillside. The middle of nowhere. A magical place that supposedly isn't. They are hiding, not wishing to be seen, like children, playing at being invisible.

Matt is lean and limber, breathing through the stress which he thinks of as excitement. He's good looking with a sharp fade of a haircut, choice diamond ear stud and body easy in its clothes. He could be just out of the army or the stylish end of a hippy festival. A quick glance at the watch tells him the other vehicle is late.

Where the fuck is this place anyway? Jesus it's quiet. A bird chirruped as if to mock the thought.

When they'd done the google maps and what3words thing and chosen it as a zero-risk location he hadn't thought anything more about it, but the quiet is creepy and he feels like he is being watched and judged even by the hedge and that tall tree over there. Season. Eggshell. Nervous. Three words to describe a place without any direct reference to it. Useful, no doubt but strangely obscuring the meaning of either the words or the place, combining them into a complex dynamic by the spell of sound. The grass blade that is now a shell, a branch called nerv. An unexpected explosion of bird from branch makes him jump. It's a sudden central shock as if a force might erupt from the top of his head. As a little boy it happened a lot. Especially after his Mum died. It's a sudden up and down slam, the stomach rises, is suspended for a sickening moment then lurches down upon itself with all the forces of gravity. A horrified reality of fear forces itself into each desperate breath, unpredictable as a storm hurtling through a landscape. Sometimes he can surf it and the feeling of free fall is devoid of anything. Sometimes not.

He checks his phone impatiently. The wave passes.

Finally, the approach of another car roaring from down the lane.

It draws up, engine idling. There's no banter, just the exchange through the window and then it's all done and gone.

The clunk shut of the car boot and door, the ignition fired up and now he's away.

Driving back to town where he'll deliver and receive his pay. All very simple really. That sudden jumpy thing recedes back in the comfort of foot on pedal, arm controlling the gears and loud rap. The words of the songs make sense to him. They're painful.

Gravity is what appears to make things heavy, falling downwards as they will through space on earth. Its force tries to pull two things towards each other, the more massive, the greater the pull. The heavier a thing is, the faster it gets to you.

Up in the garden Karen was sitting quietly next to the clothing which dangled limply on the line. The cat had jumped up onto her lap. She was looking over at the horizon when the car drew up. She was expecting a parcel and waited for the squeak of the gate and the delivery man to come up the steps. It was such an out of the way place, you wouldn't know the cottage was there from the lane; it was sometimes difficult to find, and parcels often went missing or simply got thrown over the hedge in desperation. Swathes of bracken and nettle almost hid the front gate of the cottage surrounded as it was by upland common.

The living on a common gave her a feeling of liberty, an ancestral whisper of a time before the idea of land ownership was even a twinkle in a would-be acquirer's eye. It was anathema, non sensical. How could anybody take possession of its immensity? As the source of life land is a living being propagating the nature that is our bodies as well as the hills and plains, something that can never be possessed: that we feed and live from as a mother. All original people know this. Enclosure and ownership protagonists with self-gratification bubbling in their power cauldrons, willed otherwise. After all the tussles of local land grabbing had subsided and travelled overseas to continue the colonial project it became unclear under whose ownership this common had eventually ended up. It was finally bequeathed to the local parish, in a benevolent game of pass the parcel by the lord of the manor. While squatting commoners were then as threatened a species as curlew or nightingale are now, they became the 'landless' and were no longer actively engaged in communal husbandry being forced to work either for the new landlords or to travel to the cities to find minimum wage work. By dint of owning enough acreage generationally established landowning families perhaps believed themselves to be the rightful beneficiaries of what was once held in common yet as a pile of manure steams in its decomposition, so the memories of what is rightful also break down. A couple of hundred years later, in a fine display of timeless transmutable energy, a neighbouring estate owned by another lord of a manor, would rent out a discarded farmhouse where the harvested crop that Matt was waiting to pick up would be grown. The crop would be used to quell the wrongness of the arrangement in both the oppressor and the oppressed.

Standing sentinel at the back gate onto the common behind the cottage a Yew tree of indeterminate age shades the ground beneath its mighty being. Darkened by the deep green shadow of its feathered needles, the dense iron wood is red and the dreaming in its trunk and roots contours like a frozen glacier. It is quiet in this dark aura as if the weight of deep space is gathered listening and is not to be interrupted. Everything ancient has in fact endured, it has concentrated its wisdom, challenging death. It will be part of the dismantling of the present arrangements, but patience is at its heart. It will wait until the great swathes of cyclical time click to a point of correct alignment. Ownership, non-ownership, common, uncommon none of this applies. Ultimately the land will deliver its own truth.

Alongside the Yew a fence line delineates the garden that Karen tended. No delivery driver appeared in her garden. Karen decided against going down and poking her head over the gate nosily. 'Karen' had recently become an insult. She had briefly considered changing her name to Ka. Then thought better of it as pretentious. Human beings trapped in their own self-importance and judgment can be such ignorant animals and with so much given away to the omnipotent intelligence of the machine, almost imbecilic. Unlike the intelligence of cats, she thought, absentmindedly stroking the soothing fur.

There was the noise of another car, another moment shunted by and then both cars were gone as the stillness of the morning returned.

She came here from a big city. Oblivious to any local politics or history, longing for the relative freedom of the hillside, the lack of noisy or nosy neighbours, she found the closer contact with nature, the quietly wild and elevated corner had initially offered her solace and solitude.

But all around were sheep who grazed the overburdened pasture on the common, desperately coughing and limping, they were pitiable specimens of commodification. Their fleeces were splattered with farmers' colours, a tawdry heraldry of coloured spots to describe ownership. It had become unprofitable to always shear them so sometimes their fleeces were left to slowly tear away from the skin as if they were not quite managing to take off their clothes and the occasional view of a scrawny neck or revealing skinny leg suggested they were little more than a farmers' cast-off whores. Karen found it hard to witness this style of animal husbandry and took care to notice if a lamb or ewe was badly struggling. She would notify the farmer when the stench of a rotting corpse alerted her to the demise of yet another poor creature. She ranted quietly to herself, impotent in the face of brutalised market forces and conflicted by the conditioned cruelty she saw all around her. The farmers were forced to operate on a scale that was inherently depersonalising; if the economy of scale didn't care, why should anyone else? The local abattoir down in the valley was routinely fined for polluting the rivers with blood and guts and endless chemicals involved in the killing process. Paying the penalty was cheaper than purifying the process in good old England. Little wonder rats were prospering.

Karen had thought about keeping chickens but then decided against it because of attracting these cunning creatures. She had learned the hard way about their clever ways. Perhaps as an initiation into rural living they had shown and tested her with their versatility and prowess. Rats are everywhere. They can chew through all manner of materials, squeeze their adaptable bodies in between the tiniest of apertures and have photographic visual memories that work out the floor plan and instigate the strategic assault on the human fortress. Via the darkest tunnels they manage to breach the human defences of walls, floors and roofs to storm the castle and win dominion over your life. When fetid rat shit was spattered around her kitchen and the fruit in the bowl serrated by incisor's troughs Karen knew she had been overrun. She was forced to take in a couple of supposedly feral cats, soon discovering their company to be superior to much of the human variety. Cats became her love, their feline wisdom soothed and excited her, their liquid movement showed her a way of flexibility she had rarely felt within herself, and they protected her from invasion with the merciless pursuit and slaughter of the hunt.

One rat, battle weary from close encounters with these predators, sat cautiously under cover of plentiful bushes, looking on with the cold distance of a mercenary. Her yellowed in pointing- incisors flicked in and out of focus with the rhythm of the twitch of her whiskers. The dull brown fur grew in angles away from an agile nose and parted around the gleaming black pebbles of her eyes. Her long worm like tale spilled out from a plump body, she was pregnant and incontinent. She and her brood had had to adapt now the cats lived here. The human was alright, there was food in the compost bin, they wouldn't starve.

Matt returned home calmed by the reassuring concentration of driving. The power of foot on accelerator and the rhythmic synchronicity of gear changing gave him a feeling of control in the security of the confines of the warm car. Driving was a skill he considered himself good at. Something he could relax about without doubt constantly lurking.

He had always had to be self-reliant and that had only got more defined the older he became. Not that he was old. Knocking on 30 isn't exactly old, is it? But he had decided on a quiet night in. Now as he prepared to roll the spliff he was ready for the altered state the smoke gave him. Patting his pockets, he searched for the small bag of grass he'd had with him in case he had gone out to party. He searched through his jacket then realised it was gone. Never mind someone else's lucky day, plenty more where that came from.

His flat was small, functional, and devoid of any homely touches. He kept it clean, a barren antiseptic cleanliness without the sparkle of the pure. Old smoke hung in the air lurking around the soft cushioning of the sofa with the grim determination of a stalker. Sometimes he opened the windows, but the wailing of sirens and the neighbours' domestic arrangements amplified what he didn't want to hear so mostly the windows stayed shut and the air compromised. The sounds outside churned on regardless behind the double-glazed panes which were milky with trapped moisture obscuring clear sight. The small city was big enough for a degree of anonymity yet small enough for a nod and hello from the neighbours. Matt was cautious with all interactions, but they knew him now in the local shop, and sometimes the girl he liked was there on the till and that made a difference to a day.

She was kind looking and even though he didn't know if he fancied her, she looked him directly in the eye and would smile and he liked that.

He took a deep lungful, held it in then exhaled allowing the depth of the breath to relax him, the broccoli alveoli of lung laced with THC meeting the tributary rivers of blood. Yeah, the drop had all gone according to plan. Another successful mission and enough cash to tide him over till the next time. Another deep draw in and annoyingly with it came that horrible empty feeling he sometimes encountered. The 'is this it then' moment. It had been occurring more often recently. Another inhale and rush to move away from that void into a numb zone. Put the music on. This time some dub reggae that filled in the background with a soothing pulse.

Ok, he was off and safely away from the inside of him.

His thoughts slid to the girl, her smile. He'd ask her out. Just for a coffee or a stroll. Didn't want to seem desperate or anything. Then they were in the park, and it was sunny. Gradually the longing for the fantasy of her and a deep yearning for togetherness consumed him.

But as the smoke spiralled it conjured a palace. Leaving the park, he was aware the palace offered both the height of pleasure and the depths of deception and despair. The twist was in the decision. Here you could either let your hair down, relax and enjoy everything on offer or else be thrown into a dungeon horror ride of paranoia seemingly limited only by imagination and chemistry.

You take your pick. It is a free will planet.

He didn't know what would happen when he crossed the threshold. Perhaps a saucy smile, sometimes an edge of sharpened tooth, threatening to bite. Sternly penetrating, control will be toppled with punishment from a dark and insidious mind, or the thermals will whisk you high as a kite buzzing on the winds of creation itself.

Suddenly a burlesque theatre's plush velvet curtains swooped, maroon swagged, to frame the seductive image of a dream lover lying beckoning, legs akimbo, taut, muscular, plump or juicy, whatever you fancy invited the upholstery, before morphing wildly into a concrete inquisition room, unwindowed and airless, where eyes were blinded, a violent glare burning out retinas, echoing whispers in darkened corners.

Searching freedom of flight, the numbing of wounds, the blackmailing of senses, to erase inhibition and blot the ink stain of shameful unbearable memories through ever shifting landscapes. Take this plant in and it will only allow certain persons of lineage to receive gifts unblemished. It's a complicated protocol that many have forgotten. Either way, you will learn if you're willing to encounter the vagaries of an unknowable payback scheme.

Nothing comes without something else happening, pain is never simply banished, take your chances, and be sure it's a chance you are taking, a choice you're making. A gamble with unknowable odds. Snoozing on the job can prove dangerous. As pain increases so does the need for diversion and the plant is becoming plump on the calls on its abundance. The joint now spent; it is extinguished in the grit grey ashtray.

Chapter two

Karen keeps her cottage garden neat and tidy. It's the least she can do for her elderly landlord who lets her have the place for a pittance by today's rental standards. Besides she enjoys the gentle tending, she works on others' gardens too, it's her job. It brings in enough for her to live on simply and on her own terms. Mind you, she thinks, not many people would manage to live here.

Because the cottage is cold and damp. Single paned windows rot quietly on their sills and a dark bloom of mould lingers around patches on the wall. Multiple envelopes proclaiming government grants for insulation and improvements regularly littered the doormat, but the landlord didn't want the fuss or bother, too much upheaval, so they went unheeded.

Externally there is an earthy beauty to the stones and simple construction. It had been erected three hundred years earlier to provide shelter for quarry workers and their families as they toiled digging rock and coal for the furnaces and furtherment of industrialisation. There were no foundations as such, it stood directly on the earth of the hillside, the stones had been piled up into a structure not far from where they had been dug. Whatever you could build in a day was yours to live in as long as there was a fire blazing in the hearth by nightfall.

At times large numbers of family members had lived there: over the years children, adults and animals were all to be found living under the shelter of the one roof, one room with the inglenook fireplace downstairs and a loft space above with straw pallets for sleeping on.

Rock and stone know of heat and the pressures of ice and water. Fashioned in sculpted variations that bear witness to the vast stories of the world and its galactic neighbours, they are formed in endurance. Silently they shift at an imperceptible pace whilst appearing inert and insensitive. Occasionally the immense forces that forged the very structure of earth, buck and rear up in quaking rebellion. Mostly they hold stable in the infinitely slow cycles of change that a rock exists through, its lifetime a baffling infinity if you're not one.

Outside the cottage's charming rustic appeal spellbinds the modern eye. The close quarters of its industrial heritage, the short lives worn out by hard labour apparently evaporate, it appears now like a chocolate box vignette in a brochure promoting nostalgia.

A small brickwork extension had doubled its size at the beginning of the twentieth century, providing kitchen, bathroom and small extra bedroom.

Karen loved the situation, the dancing ravens, the wheeling kites, squabbling rooks and expansive colours of uncluttered skies that lit distant hills beyond the valley where trees and field and hedge were drawn in varying densities of shade upon the contoured land. An unusual wind occasionally blew into the bird's eye view, playing with the visual story, murmuring quietly of the collapse of time, echoing what we casually refer to as past and over. The denial of the present as densely compacted as the clay of the hill. It wasn't only the sheep who were suffering, sometimes she saw deep unease and unhappiness etched into human faces passing in the lane and the postures of peoples' bodies walking dogs on the common or out shopping in town as packets of food trebled in price and diminished in size. There was both a frenzy and a profound stillness digging a hole in the same moment. Into which some people seemed to be falling.

Her personal story and the narrative held in the stones of her dwelling resonated a legacy tinged with compromise, a photograph faded by light just managing to hold enough colour to still contrast one thing from another yet losing sufficient definition for vaguely remembered detail to be decipherable.

She lived alone, managing financially on her meagre income but grateful enough for the limited freedom it allowed. Somehow however, it felt less than she had hoped for as if she had been cheated out of a win on the lottery or a birth right of happiness.

Her only son didn't get in touch with her anymore, not even with a card at Christmas.

Perhaps she should never have given him that ultimatum. But it had made sense at the time. He needed to hear her side of the story. She couldn't understand how he hadn't seen through the manipulation of his father. Any responsibility the man had perhaps once felt had vaporised the evening he had walked out of the door. But then he had set about ensnaring the affections of his son, luring him away from her, the mother, and occasionally a hot sulphuric fury still burned when she thought about him as the cheating bastard whom she found it impossible to forgive.

They had never resolved anything between themselves, the acrimony had merely ossified, and their son had chosen him and his new family life over her.

Boys need their dads he had sneered triumphantly.

And the mother? The mother…did she not count for anything?

With a sharp stab of regret, her own grey mother sat in the scene of her childhood quietly peeling potatoes and dusting the mantelpiece. It had never occurred to Karen to sympathise with her, she had found her pathetic. It was a hopeless wasteful river down which the mothers were washed away. It was a bitter bridge they flowed under, the sweetest maternal feelings drowned by anger and resentment.

There didn't seem to be any point in hoping for reconciliation now. The last glimmer had been a phone call with a faraway voice a few years before. Asking politely after how she was. Tentative, quiet. They had even managed through those few initial pleasantries and then she'd apparently said the wrong thing: saying she missed him or something like it.

'Why do you always have to blame everyone else and play the victim? Dad's right, I shouldn't have bothered.' Shouting, he had left the call and the click of disconnection rang through her ears. Scoured by blame and accusation, a horribly familiar injustice had opened the same old wound: to feel eternally in the wrong. It had been like returning to sniff at something fetid just to remind herself of the stench.

Sweeping the final plant clippings into a neat pile, she stooped down to scoop them up then went to throw them into the compost heap.

The rat sighed, what did this woman know of being reviled.

The sickly-sweet smell of rotting emanated from the bin as the lid was opened. She was entranced by the way things broke down, glancing into the decay, she chose to ignore the rathole and the giveaway signs of chewed process within. The rats were welcome to it. The feline huntress had her killing sprees and sometimes the kites would swoop down onto the lawn, wingspan massive and finely choreographed to retrieve an unwanted carcass. The warm shelter of the compost bin was fair game for the rat's share.

Wilfully she would leave a lemon on the worktop to watch its quiet disintegration at the mercy of the mould. She enjoyed watching the yellow green bloom white as it enveloped the fruit leaving a fine dust as if in a dream of itself.

That'll be all that's left. Then the silvered slug trails wound through the dust, casting a random patina on the work surfaces as spores of the mould circulated, creating invisible clouds in the air.

It was a long time since anyone other than rodents, slugs, mould and now the cats, had shared her kitchen, her experiments with wedges of bread and encrusted plates had literally mushroomed. She gave them free reign. It was a delightful negligence; deliciously disgusting. Her mother's mantra *You don't want to be thought a common slut* bought an ironic smile to her face.

She wasn't even naturally messy but these days as soon as anyone inferred anything about how she should behave she was on them like a shark at the peak of its evolutionary cycle: unrequired to explain itself. In many other respects she was carefully scrupulous: brushing her still auburn hair almost religiously, she then would clear the brush of its moulting and knot the fibres into a clump before throwing it from the bathroom window for the birds to use in their springtime nests. Little delighted her more than to find these strands of hair carefully woven into the mossy sticks, leaves and feathers entangled in a nest by skilful beaks. She could imagine herself transformed by feathered wings, resting in their comfort.

And she did enjoy a certain self-disciplined order to her days. When out working she left early with a flask and a sandwich, the routine of preparation having soothed and reassured her. But mostly domestic affairs were haphazard, as there weren't many people with whom she felt close anymore, no one to care for her nor she for them. Not any who would be bothered to comment on her behaviour. The lack of active family bonds detached her from past and future. Friends from earlier days were closing in on themselves, becoming increasingly distant as topics of health-related conversation narrowed their minds with physical concerns, replacing earlier adventures or relationship scandals with pharmaceutical lists and hospital appointments. Funny how age did that. People losing each other to death and disease. Just when you thought you had escaped the past, the accumulation of too many linear expectations concertinaed like a motorway pile up, inevitably reaching a point of crushing fragmentation.

She had been actively interested in personal development, attended workshops seeking guidance from teachers of various traditions who genuinely seemed to want to help. Crystal healing, astrological constellations, counselling, tarot divination, spirit mediumship, silent meditation. They had all intrigued her yet somewhere along the way she had simply run out of steam, lost in the eternal efforts to surrender to pain. But it didn't go away. Feeling therefore defeatedly, obliged to throw the babies out with bathwater her tolerance had evaporated, and she was left with little to truly care for and an emptiness that was guarded by the pretence of welcome autonomous solitude.

Her friend Nancy, met long ago on a gardening course had recently moved far enough away for a quick tea or lunch date to be impossible.

'You should get out more darling,' she suggested on a now rare phone call, 'how about online dating?' Karen snorted, neither convinced nor inclined to risk it.

They used to drive halfway between their homes to visit a garden or visitor centre, but differing opinions set up by the government guidelines of the preceding years had wedged an undebatable gap between them. Now that nothing seemed negotiable the challenges of meeting up became nearly impossible to overcome. And there was Nancy's husband, a solicitor who insisted on knowing everything about all possible subjects so an invitation to visit their home was like pulling teeth and of course he would know all about that too having wondered about dentistry as a possible career. Nor was Nancy interested in schlepping up to hers and slumming it in relative squalor. All these were the reasons to resign from effort.

'Darling it's too much' she had said when Karen had suggested a weekend together. Gone were the days when they had laughed together like schoolgirls stifling giggles or exploding in naughty merriment when an observation became absurd, or a passing inanity was momentarily framed. As the joy vanished so the care steadily eroded.

Her other closest friend, a bold and outspoken woman whom she had admired for her eggshell crushing humour had seemed to betray her in a complex chain of intricate chess moves which had been nigh on impossible to understand let alone unravel. She had been left feeling as if a snake were writhing in her psyche manipulating her emotional synapses, somehow fundamentally at fault for allowing her own honesty to be expressed. Where is our power if not in our truth? She had been angry. But kindness is also necessary, and it had hidden away when she looked for it in the bare cupboards of her heart. It was simpler to break contact. A lot is made of the breakup of marriages or intimate sexual relationships, it's understood there is pain and bereavement when they are lost. But when a trusted friendship is devastated by complicated battling manoeuvres an equally painful ragged hole is left, a shot gun wound in the social web that also ricochets around any bystanders.

Still, she had her neighbours and a small but friendly circle of acquaintances in town if she wanted to go out for the evening. She would never have admitted it, least of all to herself but sometimes her preference for solitude was impossible to discern from a habitual and deep-rooted loneliness. She checked the kitchen clock. It was a reasonable time to open a bottle of wine. She had some standards dictated by an untraceable code of decorum around alcohol, beneath which lay a vague feeling of ruin dissolved by the first glass.

Karen's was only one of thousands of bottles of wine bought from the mecca of the supermarket aisles then consumed each night throughout the nation. Within each of those glass bottles the essence of 700 or so grapes floats waiting to be uncorked, fruity genies contemplating the fulfilment of everyone's wishes. The trouble with the first glass was it inevitably led to the second. What exactly was she gazing into past the slender neck through the glass cylinder's depths? She enjoyed red wine, a little snifter as she put it, thinking that sounded jokingly sophisticated. The dark red juice sometimes stained her mouth and tasted simultaneously of strength and languor, its bitter sweetness spurring her on to relax until she consequently felt very present, sharpened like a blade on a steel. The cut needed no effort until it suddenly blunted blurring at the edges whilst she, merging with the fermented grape, leant on an angle poised palm. Time was when she was a storytelling dancer throughout whole nights and kept going the rest of the next day. She mused on the characters she'd caroused with, wine had been her life blood, had led to the abandon of sex with whoever was sharing the bottle, decadent in nonchalance. She twisted a long strand of unruly hair, still lush and full: grape vines entwine seductively, their leaves drape and tendrils curl in the warmth of a climate where conviviality prospers. If the fruits of these vines, the rituals of sociability, and the invitation of the grape towards insight were all bound by the process of fermentation and the skill of the alchemist vintner, why then this current bouquet of lonely bitterness? Now she drank steadily, running from her questions to sink gently into a quicksand puddle of cheer, despondency, nostalgia and besottedness. The genie grants the wish, she must simply be careful what she wishes for.

◻

Matt woke with a start, his mouth furred with the flavour of ashtrays. It was dark but the yellow light of the streetlamps crept through the curtains into the fog of his mind. There was nothing of comfort in the room, so he shut his eyes again to absorb the absence. There was his heart beating, here the cramp of his shoulder against the hard edge of sofa. His feet were cold, and a huge ache swelled in his throat. He wanted to howl but the neighbours would hear. This slow and excruciating struggle was what he thought all life was about. Containing a dark oppressive force. Putting on a battle mask to wear outside. There was nobody he could tell it to. He didn't know there was any route other than through a harsh cold colourless corridor.

He was only eight when she had died. Before that as far as he could remember it had seemed ok, normal. He had been normal, with friends, and then school and a life kicking about then going home. He had been part of something. Not that it was perfect. There was the troubling unknown space of a dad.

But he wasn't alone with that.

His mum had been the one. The soft place where he belonged. She had sorted everything, made them a home, cared about what happened to him.

Then there came the days when she couldn't get up out of bed, the weird smell of their little flat. The way she got so skinny and yellow. Her eyes and teeth becoming huge in her face, as she looked at him with such deep intensity he didn't want to look back. She started giving him advice. Her friends brought food round and spoke quietly. Until one evening when Sarah knocked on the door of his bedroom.

'Mind if I come in?' She was a plump woman with dark shoulder length hair that looked like it might snap if you touched it wrong. She had a lot of earrings and her clothes strained at the seams. He liked her enough but now she was in his bedroom she was too close and smelling like an unwashed frying pan.

'Your mum's not at all well darling, she's going to have to go into hospital for a bit, but you can come and stay with us. You know my girls, one's in the year below you, Mrs Dermott's class, they'll be very happy to have you stay at ours.'

He'd been silent. Not knowing what he was supposed to say until he thought to ask when. 'We'll take her in tomorrow morning. They told us today there was a bed had come available for her. I'll pick you up after school and we'll go and visit once she's settled in. It'll be like a little holiday.' She smiled gently but he couldn't look at her for long. He knew that you didn't go to hospital for a holiday, it was confusing.

Thankfully she was getting up now and leaving the room because he could feel a strange spinning inside himself as if he was being pulled up towards the ceiling through the vortex of a tornado. The click of the bedroom door sounded as if it came from another planet and the padding of her feet down the stairs a foreign noise that was uninterpretable. His heart was thumping but he wasn't inside himself to feel the blood pulse. His mum's weak voice called from the other side of the wall.

'Come in here Matty love.'

A shade of sticky darkness had swooped down and slid into the cracked shield of his little being.

Shadow might be cast by light and joy defined by suffering but a tender child without protection learns to distrust.

Chapter three

When he opened his eyes again dawn was filtering through the window nullifying the jaundiced street with the cold blue of morning. Another night on the sofa over. Another day to shift through. A poster for a martial arts class had caught his eye the other day on his way home from the shops. The sessions were starting down the road and something about the flier had engaged him. It looked as if it had been hand drawn, with a little figure flying over the lettering. A small voice urged him: there was nothing to lose. And if there was one asset he did have, it was a good body. He'd been training down at the gym and couldn't help comparing his physique to some of the other blokes there. He noticed the puffed-up ones whose muscles would turn to fat in an instant if they didn't keep their regimes going regularly. He knew how to handle himself and his body responded quickly and with ease to most situations that required strength or agility. He was proud of that and reckoned that the class might give him a chance to prove himself. The trouble with the gym was it was all machines, cold metal, beeps and plastic moulding. Although his dad was a blank space, Matt's body was most definitely a genetic similar. If his mum had even considered it, she had not spoken of him, nor of the fact that shortly after she became pregnant, he had disappeared. The rumours of crack and mugging didn't encourage her memory. there was no one to recognise as he grew into a miniature replica of his dad. It was back in the day when most people still cashed their pensions and benefits at a post office. He had circled like a hawk eyeing up vulnerable prey, following a likely candidate down into the quieter streets then swooping to snatch a bag or wallet from behind, jogging easily away with the booty stuffed into his jacket until he was out of range and could stroll again.

One day an elderly lady had resisted and hung on to her handbag and he had felled her, hearing the thud of her skull as it cracked on the pavement. He'd grabbed the bag from her falling arm and sprinted away fast into a neighbouring street. He was just beginning to calm his gasping breath when from behind two big chasing blokes had jumped him and brought him down. They'd sat on his arms and chest until the police arrived, the handbag matching him without doubt to the dying woman. Sent down for 6 years for manslaughter he then vanished into emptiness.

Matt had got so used to denying a dad's existence. Having an unknown quantity where others had a father was a quandary when he was first at school. Plenty of kids had dads who didn't live with them, but it was the total absence that made it difficult to make anything up. His mum had maybe thought it best to protect him from the gossip and associated shame, he didn't know, she hadn't said. He had felt it as a tightrope, potentially super cool with some but by others he was undermined: despite themselves they couldn't help but ostracise illegitimacy. In that way his mum's death had saved him any further explanations as he had simply become an orphan. At some point in those shocking years after moving on from the first foster parents he had taken up smoking, it had been a link to her, a way to hold her hand.

Rolling your own was something to do with your hands. It gave you a purpose and took up concentration while you peeled the rizla from the slot in its little neat cardboard package pulling out a string of the conker-coloured threads and rolling a cylinder careful to tuck in the edge of the fine paper before running your tongue along the gum. There was satisfaction to be had. Each time the lighter wheel spun a spark, and the flame lit the rollie's end, before you'd even taken a draw, there was ritual. It took attention, gave you an activity and then later adding a bit of blow meant you could hang out with people without too much serious interaction other than hilarious observations on mundane absurdities. This kept him within a group of pals though they never spoke of anything else.

Although he didn't want to admit it, he had lately started to feel the smoking taking its toll on his breathing. If he was honest, it now seemed more trouble than it was worth, but habits die hard. And nicotine is highly addictive. All the pain was kept down by repeated rolling, lightings and breathing ins. Matt wouldn't yet explain it to himself like that, but he was aware of a churning discontent with the repetitive sameness of all the smoking rituals, the paraphernalia, the aftertaste and smell on his breath, the tightening in his chest cavity as if a ravenous creature was rumbling in revolt in his lungs, calling for attention amidst a fog of constant suppression.

Time was when everyone smoked, in pubs, on trains, even in special bits of hospital wards. Squinting through swathes of spiralling smoke was no longer considered cool and now the vapes had arrived it was old fashioned to be burning tobacco when you could suck on a battery powered plastic thing flavoured like a sweet.

It was not something that Matt knew that the smoke of tobacco could send prayers to a great creator spirit. In its plant wisdom power, peace and agreement could plume towards the sky, carrying messages from the heart brokering communication while offerings of reciprocity and exchange could be carried in pouches. Desecrated and commodified, tobacco use wreaks havoc with the health of millions, decimating the hearts, lungs, and circulatory systems of people everywhere. Matt's mum had been one of those statistics.

Despite plenty of opportunity Matt had never bothered with other heavier drugs. It gave him the edge for his work. He was known to be clearheaded and reliable and was allotted the distribution drops that needed someone who could be responsible. These days he only smoked a bit of weed after work when the job was done. He didn't want to know what happened to those who, persuaded by their own addictions, disobeyed the orders, when the need for stimulation or suppression overtook them. He just understood it wasn't pretty. He wasn't supposed to be at work again for another three days, so the Kung Fu class was well timed. Yes, he'd call in there later, it had said all welcome on the notice. Something about it gave him a glimmer of clean excitement. It was a long time since he'd looked forward to anything.

The Kung Fu class was in an old school gym that had been repurposed as a community centre. Garish lettering announced its aims and objectives on peeling posters beneath high windows which started above their heads. The glass panes slanted rectangles of evening light over the yellow, red and white lines that criss-crossed the floor. Attachable punch bags in faded mock leather dangled at strategic places along the back wall which was braced with wooden bars that could be pulled out for climbing up.

The teacher was only slightly older than Matt and had the easy, attractive gait of a big cat walking loosely in its skin. A huge grin cracked an otherwise impassive face as he greeted the class of assembled students. They were all ages, shapes and sizes. Instantly Matt felt at ease. As if a door was opening into something unknown yet familiar that he hadn't realised he'd been yearning for. In the first few moments of practice breathing, a gentle space opened up inside him, there was room for life to course through him where restriction had been blocking it. The pace was energetic, centred around postures and applications of principles of attack and defence. Parry and punch, block and advance. Deep in his bones or even in the more complex strands of genetic material Matt knew this dance. It was familiar. It was light and fluid. The teacher noticed and encouraged him cheerfully,

'Moving with flow isn't a belief system, it's a direct felt experience. Soften your belly, let the breath fill it, this is your powerhouse.' He slapped his slim but rounded belly, 'use the leverage of the floor to move with and boom, out it comes through your limbs.' He laughed as he threw a whip of a kick into the space with apparently no effort. Matt was impressed. He copied.

'Good. Now try to align your body with heaven and earth and turn like a wheel. All the energy of the universe is at your disposal.'

He was shown how to position shoulders and hips stacked in alignment, to move as a unified unit of power.

Two hours flew by, and Matt knew that what he'd been shown could become a daily practice. No problem. Exhilarated he went up to the teacher.

Gus reached out a warm hand and they shook. 'Coming for a drink?' Matt found himself declining out of habit.

'Perhaps next time then,' said Gus, gently touching him on the arm as they parted company on the pavement outside the hall.

A surge of joy billowed through him ending at his face where he caught it and grinning, sauntered away down the street.

◻

The bottle empty, Karen didn't feel anything but morose, the red grapes' magic soured in her belly. She looked at the little bag of grass as if it was a dubious museum specimen. It was a long time since she had smoked anything. This little crumpled bit of plastic she had found down by the pull in on the lane. Picking it up as litter it had surprised her to be full of buds and leaves. She had thrown it on the table. Now she spoke aloud, a soft slurring whine. 'To hell with it.' Careful, thought the stone walls, hearing the lonely voice. There was a small clay pipe balanced in a cleft of one of the fireplace stones. She had dug it from the garden early on in her time here and had been thrilled to find it intact. Now she took it from its small hollow and filled the bowl with the dried leaves. She drew carefully on the slender stem so as not to burn her mouth or lips. The smoke invaded her like a snake, slithering down her throat challenging her not to cough. She held it in as long as she dared then spluttering, released it back out into the room, no longer a thin streak but now an amorphous cloud. Repeating this a couple more times she had an irresistible urge to lie down and reached the horizontal moments before she would have crashed there unconscious.

Young Karen had arrived in London after leaving the nondescript parental home of a featureless suburbia and the dull stifling claustrophobia of know your place and don't step out of line. Her mum and dad's conformity had made her want to scream. Watching her dutiful elder brother obey triggered automatic resistance, she wanted away from this. So she had run.

Willowy, tall and with a shock of auburn curls her deep brown eyes sparkled with feral attraction. Her parents shook their heads in despair fearing her to be a fallen woman, wanton, a shame of which they could never be proud, why was she like that and not like them? Her presence seemed to evoke the forest in a building, she naturally embodied a revolutionary impulse, as if the evils of waywardness that brought about the collapse of structure followed her like a pack of wild dogs. Her way was natural, as unpredictable as a summer storm, her appetite that of a predator. When she hit the city, her wildlife properly ignited, the beige parents fading away to almost forgotten. Those days she had worked in what is now called hospitality. Back then it was called front of house or waitressing and bar work. There was an art to putting people at their ease and enjoying serving them that she found came as second nature and it wasn't difficult to pick up tips, so the money was decent enough.

Every now and then a little gang of fellow workers would nip out for a breath of fresh air and share joints beside the extractor fan that cleared the rancid cooking vapours from the kitchen. It was as fresh as city air got and they laughed at the euphemism and checked the mirrors in the staff toilets for signs of intoxication before going back out to the theatre of the café bar where no one seemed any the wiser. Work had been fun then.

Bill came in with a group of after work diners and he'd stared at her as though she had appeared from heaven. Completely entranced, he had courted her with the devotion of a parasite. Dependent and ever present. She couldn't have been less interested. She was popular and had a stream of willing lovers, but her indifference only seemed to fuel his ardour. She became a prize to be won. And so, he wore her down with the persistence of a rodent, gnawing away at any resistance. Eventually his passion persuaded her into a pattern that she failed to recognise as the conventional imprisonment of her childhood. The secure feeling of having someone so devoted to her had ultimately succeeded in seducing her and it wasn't long before she was pregnant. They were thrilled and innocently delighted that their love could make another. They giggled together as her belly swelled with innocence, the dome protruding with the elbows and legs stretches of the growing embryo. His hands stroked and caressed the mound of their future child.

But the grinding open of her pelvis to deliver a purplish slithery creature into the world had deeply shocked her.

She hadn't been prepared for the hormonal roller coaster of it all. She had loved her little baby in a way that was disturbing to her, had felt helpless and incapable yet so responsible for the little being of him, but he had cried so much, and she couldn't always soothe him, and the exhaustion of sleeplessness felt less like a night out on the tiles and more like a marathon when you were a heavy smoker.

It was relentlessly demanding, and Bill became increasingly unsympathetic. He had looked at her as if surprised to see her floundering then left to sleep in the other room so he 'wouldn't disturb her'. His passionate declarations of undying love vanished as swiftly as her sleep patterns. Bereft of support she had felt this betrayal as keenly as her parents probably had her own. Silently she punished him and when she spoke it was with a sharp-edged scorn that seemed her only defence against a cavernous void.

Whilst everyone in their fast-evaporating social circle assumed they were this newly loved up little family a huge frozen sadness had swept like a tidal wave over her, a dark drowning had waterlogged her soul with loss. There wasn't anyone she could explain it to. It was both too heavy and indefinable. It seemed as if there was no real reason for the detachment she crawled around in, groping for a recognisable compass reading.

Family life was a few years of strategic compromise based on the unfolding needs of the little one as the three of them remained together. There was little intimacy which seemed to suit them both. His parents lived abroad so were as good as absent. Hers played minor roles in a sad drama of convention when birthdays and holidays dictated.

Then one day she started to come up for air, feeling the weight of thawing water start to stream from her shoulders, a cross channel swimmer finally catching sight of land.

Jimmy was in a playgroup a couple of mornings a week and the simple rhythm of life was no longer so stultifying, was almost comforting. She remembered the early spring morning with crystalline clarity when she had looked at Bill with a softened gaze and felt a surge of affection as she watched him put their child's coat on his wriggling little body, threading arms through sleeves and fastening the zip with the noise of whistle. He had returned her gaze quizzically but without the defensiveness she had come to expect. Perhaps they could manage after all, a kernel of hope pulsed, daring itself to swell and burst forth.

While they were out, she had bathed and scented her skin and hair and rubbed moisturiser into the skin of her face and neck in an act of self-love that had been so recently eroded, it was a delicious and purposeful revelation to recover herself. There was no doubt she was a beautiful woman and the sacrificial years of the demands of motherhood, had only intensified that beauty, sculpted as it was by experience. She took a deep breath. Ready to re-emerge and return to herself, a diffident sense of deep love for the man who was the father of her child fluttered cautiously in the crysalis, a butterfly unfurling newly formed wings.

Perhaps the discovery might not have been so devastating had it not been for these precious moments of seeming rebirth.

Perhaps her hatred might not have been felt with such venom had she never felt herself resurfacing after all.

Perhaps she might have been able to harness those first treasures of recollection to simply let him go, but it hadn't played out that way. The shock of humiliating rejection had hit her too forcefully, she didn't get to recover.

When Bill and Jimmy returned from their trip to the park after playgroup she had been waiting with snacks and a smile. Her internal shift had been so seismic it was a surprise he didn't seem to have noticed, but she bided her time. After Jim was snuggled in for the night they had been in the habit of a review of the day and the schedule for the next like efficient nursing staff handing over on a shift.

'What say we have a drink?' she had suggested shyly this evening.

'I don't think so Karen, I've got an early start and besides there's no point in it is there really?' He spoke with such certainty.

'How do you mean?' She had asked, still innocent and openly expectant.

'Well, we both know it's a charade don't we, you can't seriously think there's any point in having a drink together, as if there's anything left to salvage after the time we've had? Jimmy's the only reason we're both still here and we both know it. I've been meaning to talk to you about how best to rearrange our set up, so I suppose in a way now's as good a time as any.'

'What do you mean rearrange?'

'Well Lisa and I would like to be able to live together, she's waited a long time. Been really very patient while I did the right thing by you and Jimmy but now it's time for us to have things our way for a change'

'Who the hell is Lisa?'

'You can't be serious that you had no idea we were getting involved Karen. I mean, come on she's been working at the playgroup since Jim first started there, I've been raving about her forever.'

'This is unbelievable Bill. Since when did I know about a Lisa? As if it's completely rational and logical that you would be unfaithful, and I was supposed to know all about it? Listen to yourself!' Her breath was staggering between words, the pitch rising.

'Listen to yourself,' he mimicked cruelly, 'Mrs madwoman, the cold wet fish thinks its unreasonable to be unfaithful! Not many men would have put up with you for this long, whatever it was we had died a long time ago. I find it hard to believe you seriously think otherwise. If you're going to be so difficult about it, I think I'll just go right now.'

'What? But we haven't even begun to sort it out.' A weird, strangled sound was struggling from her throat, a drowning panic rising.

'Oh, spare me the drama please!' A vindictive shout, a scrape back of a toppling chair and almost running out into the hall, he had thrown on a jacket and slammed out of the door and their life.

Karen's sleep was less slumber and more comatose anaesthesia. Headachy, she woke to the sound of gunshots and a cacophonous hullabaloo ringing out across the hillside. It sounded very close. Panicked by the noises and not yet fully awake she reached for the phone and dialled the number of the police. 'Can you hear that?' She said when the phone's automatic answering system was eventually answered by a human voice.

'I don't know what's going on in the valley. They're out there with guns shooting, they sound like a bunch of crazed murderers. Can you send someone?'

'It's probably the regular shoot Madam, all legal and above board.'

'But that's on Saturdays'.

'Today is Saturday, Madam,' said the officer on the other end of the line, adopting an increasingly patronising tone.

'What?'

'It's Saturday today, Madam.' Smug even.

Karen was stunned to silence, then, to recover herself she said 'well the noise of it today must contravene some sound pollution law, it's much louder and closer than usual, I can't think straight when it's going on and they've been at it all morning.'

'Would you like to make an official complaint Madam?' Sneering now.

'Please stop calling me Madam.'

'Give me your name and address including your postcode Madam and we'll open a case file for you and report back when an officer is on the ground there.' Goading.

'Don't make me laugh,' she said helplessly, 'I can't remember the last time we saw a copper round here. You know as well as I do, they'll be packed up and safely home tucking into game pie before any of your lot has even finished the paperwork'.

'Like I said, if you would like to file a formal complaint, I will need your information to open a case file.' Triumphant, now.

She didn't want to reveal her name and address. She'd never trusted the police. Why had she even rung them?

'I don't trust what you lot will do with my personal data, besides it's not about me.' Her voice was rising in volume.

'Unfortunately, if they're not contravening any laws which they may well not be, and you don't want to make an official complaint, there's nothing we can do. And as for data Madam, we have this number you are calling from logged in our system, I'm afraid these days there's no getting away from data sharing.' Jubilant.

She would have slammed down the phone if there had been a receiver and cradle into which it could be pounded. Instead, she stabbed the screen of her mobile to end the call. It was a nano second of triumph followed by a shock wave of shame and embarrassment.

What had got into her? Whatever it was in that bag, there was now a burning in her throat, but it wasn't just the aftereffects of hot smoke. It was the rising of bitter panic that had been background noise forever. And that refused this time to be silenced.

'Look at yourself you're a lonely wierdo who lives in a mouldy place with no contact with your son, the only person that's supposed to love you, complaining down the phone because you got drunk and stoned and wanted to tell someone you didn't know which day it was.' She'd had all her familiar low times before but never this dangerous self-hating feeling of worthlessness. Gulping down tears she ran outside to the garden and howled gulping air as if she was drowning.

The stones of the house, the tall yew, the rats, the cats, the sky, the hill, they all heard and witnessed.

Chapter four

Belle is the lovely girl who works in the local shop. She is acknowledged as lovely by most who encounter her. It is an indefinable quality that makes her so. Like a charm that emanates from around the edges of her, a fusion of kindliness and sweet adaptability. A soft cushioning quality, set in a fair complexion and grey blue eyes, allows for a brief moments' respite from harshness. But she is no push over. Her body is strong from hauling stacking trays of groceries from stockroom to shelf. She has had her share of sharp learning and is just recovering from a confusing relationship into the depths of which she had fallen and lost trust.

Matt is parked outside and opposite the shop. He sits in his car as tipping rain is blown into patterns by wind across the windscreen. The confidence of earlier in the day has dissolved in the wet, and familiar doubt is seeping through his chest and trickling down his arms to the fingers clutching the motionless steering wheel.

He has promised himself he'd do it today. He had wanted to walk into the shop and simply ask her…fancy a coffee sometime? and after the boost of the class it had seemed the most natural and obvious next step. Now here he is in danger of chickening out. It sickened him. Because this was not the first time this had happened, he couldn't handle the real-life thing. Stuff only went on in his head.

The opening of the shop door catches his peripheral vision. She is wrapping her coat around her as protection from the rain and setting off at a half jog down the street. As if on auto pilot he jumps out of the car and crosses the road just in time to come face to face with her.

'Oh hi! You just finishing?' Feigning surprise, seeming genuine.

'Yes.' She smiled, 'piss awful weather tonight though isn't it and I wore the totally wrong shoes.' She grins at the thin pumps on her feet.

'I could give you a ride home if you like.'

'Oh! I don't want to trouble you, besides aren't you on your way into the shop?'

'Only just nipping in for a loaf,' he said a little too quickly, 'really, it's no bother, it'll save you getting soaked.'

'Well, if you're sure. I don't live too far away. Shall I wait here while you get the bread?' And she ducks into a doorway peering out at the lashing downpour bouncing on slippered feet.

He is forced to go in and buy the loaf to uphold the story. But he could toast that loaf to celebrate, and it gives him a few moments to get himself under control. Inside the transaction is over quickly, and he darts back out and points her to the car, opening the door for her and then there she was sat in the seat next to him, shaking miraculous drops of water from her hair. They pattern the dashboard with dots which she wipes with an equally wet hand, grinning apologetically.

'Wet, wet, wet,' she laughs.

'Where to m'Lady' he says 'Matt' by way of introduction.

'I'm Belle,' she replies smiling, 'pleased to meet you and thanks for this.' He grins and his heart pounds.

The end of her road is only a few minutes' drive away and the journey is taken up with next left and right after the post box.

'Thanks ever so.' Opening the car door, she is about to be gone.

Now or never….

'Would you like to grab a coffee sometime? It'd be nice to meet up if you fancy'…His face burns with the effort as his words tail off into silence.

'Sure, I'd like that.'

'You would?'

'Yep, why not.'

'Right well, um give me your number and we'll sort out when's a good time.'

Her phone was in her hands. They exchanged details.

It was almost a disappointment how easy it had been he thought as he drove off leaving her jumping puddles but then a couple of moments later that thought had been replaced by a sense of excited achievement. He didn't really dare to feel that two things might be going right, the class, and the girl but maybe, just maybe they would.

☐

Karen had been invited to her brother's party. He was turning a decade older overnight and hadn't been able to think of an excuse why not to include her in the gathering. She had accepted the invitation quickly before she could change her mind. It had felt a bit like clutching at straws from the bottom of a pit. After the phone call outburst with the police, she had gone back to bed and slept a long time, waking less jangled, the shooting finished, to find the duck egg blue envelope on the mat. It contained a jaunty card with photos of her brother during all the preceding decades with a swirly computer-generated border that was designed to evoke Celtic knotting.

Now as she got into her battered little car the prospect of the visit to a party was a welcome diversion and strangely relieving.

It would take a couple of hours to drive to where her brother lived in a newly built estate of executive housing where retirees with the right kinds of pension could stroll or jog to the nearby village shop which stocked the sourdough and coffee supplies that matched the demographic's breakfast needs.

Halfway enroute she realised the fuel gauge was dangerously close to red. The insistent orange petrol pump icon was flashing on off anxiously beeping by the time she reached the petrol forecourt with relief. Cars queued patiently. A couple of the pumps were cordoned off as a man worked on them.

As the queue slowly shifted, he finished his job and signalled for her to draw up.

Petrol stations are the epitome of machine culture. Subterranean crude oil is pumped through countless lines and tankers, refined and priced, emptied and refilled, siphoned, and repriced to end up nozzled into the car or van on the concrete plinth under the fabricated metal roofing. Humans are displaced, consumers are enslaved, everything gets polluted.

Shit! The pump hadn't clicked off and her party skirt was spattered with diesel, her boots doused with it.

Reeling off a wad of blue paper from the roll she wiped down most of the mess and went into shop. She explained the incident to the woman on the till who called the store manager.

Expecting an apology or perhaps to recount the circumstances once again, she was totally unprepared when the man went on the offensive.

'Have you paid for your fuel yet?'

'Er no, not yet I was waiting for something to be sorted as I really don't think I should pay for getting my clothes ruined by your broken pump, I don't mind paying for what's in the tank but not what went all over me!'

She could feel a tightness in her chest as she became aware of the lack of sympathy emanating from the man. He was relatively tall and broad-chested in the way that bordered on plump but wasn't yet. His hair the non-descript colour of an unbleached kitchen roll.

'All our pumps are fitted with an automatic cut off function.' He spoke to her as if she was an idiot, 'you must have overridden it, daydreaming.' Now a vile smile, 'so if you wouldn't mind paying for your fuel and leaving the premises promptly, I'd appreciate it before I think of charging you to clear up the mess on the forecourt.'

'But that pump was being worked on moments before I used it, it clearly wasn't fixed properly it's automatic cut off function did not work.' Karen explained managing to hold her own. Give him a few years and that mousey brown hair would thin and fall.

'Just moments before you arrived that pump was serviced and deemed to be in perfect working order. I hardly think accusing us of negligence is wise given how recently it passed its service check.'

Karen caught sight of the guy who had been working on the pump watching sheepishly from the stock room. This denial of culpability, the blatant bullying, and the overarching hardnosed treatment shocked her enough to lose momentum for her cause. Without it her argument faltered futile. The horribly familiar feeling of being alone, wronged and weakened struck her speechless as it parachuted down and smothered her. Injustice as a habitual experience, now manifesting as business sense offloading responsibility.

'But that is outrageous' she sputtered defensively scrabbling for a foothold.

The man in front of her stood motionless, patronising, staring.

'Please just pay your bill and leave, otherwise I will be forced to call the police.'

For a moment there appeared nowhere to go, she didn't want another weird encounter with police, so she found her purse and extracted her debit card waving it noncommittally over the card reader until she heard the distant beep.

The defeated part of her retreated, some may call it dissociation, to be replaced by a rage so pure as to be perfect, filling her with a current of power that lifted her arms to become those of a passionate preacher. She turned towards the man and felt her hands moving in strange circular motions, the fingers arranged in a held posture of some ancient precision stirring the invisible space between them.

'You will suffer for this wrong,' she cursed him quietly but with a force that seemed to cause the air all about him to quiver as his features drooped like molten wax and all the colour drained from him.

In that moment she could see the jumped up, pumped up little boy in him, desperate to do his job right and even felt a shimmer of pity.

The space within the shop reverberated with the power cascading from her as she opened the door and left the station getting into her car and driving away as if she was watching herself in a TV drama.

Deep beneath the oceans' bed, melted remains of animals and plants, of ancient trees and beings once alive liquefied and compressed by sediment and rocks and millions of years, the shiny black crudity we call oil shimmers. Small actions, dispelled as irrelevance, ripple unseen beyond obvious view.

☐

Belle hadn't expected that rainy day to bring her a spark of excitement. She was in a good mood today, enjoying her shift. It was simple enough work except when the computer system got complicated, but the thing she really liked was the human contact. All sorts came in. The older ones in the morning for their daily bits and pieces though often it was heart breaking to see either the spartan nature of the purchases or the replacement of groceries for a bottle of something to take the edge off.

She made it a point to find out people's names. When Gary shuffled in the odour of cloth-soaked urine wafted about in his tracks. Belle wondered what had happened for him to get into such a state. He wasn't even that old, he'd told her once how he'd been born the year Elvis had recorded his first single, but the gap-toothed dribbling smile bordered by white gunk in the cracked corners of his mouth made him appear decrepit. Whether the erosion was due to prison or a psychiatric stint or simply a hard life, it was strange to think he was only a little older than her dad. She took the crumpled cash from his grubby long finger-nailed hand and waited patiently as he laboriously loaded his shopping into a plastic bag faded as if by years in blinding sunlight, itself on the verge of disintegration.

Beryl only ever bought rich tea biscuits, tea, sugar and milk. She came in weekly mumbling to whatever it was she saw around her. Hunched over in a food smeared cardi her long grey hair straggled greasily over a collar spattered with the white flecks of dandruff.

Then there was Harold, who was always turned out with a bit of care. Even though his cuffs were frayed and shoes worn, he moved with the dignity of a cruise liner, stately and unhurried, docking into port. She wondered where he had moved from as she passed cans of ale and crisps through the scanner. Sometimes he came in with a shy lady for whom he opened the door with great chivalry as she entered eyes cast downwards as one might into a church. He held a protective hand gently at the small of her back to guide her solicitously along the aisles as if she was a trolley needing steering. On those occasions he was more likely to buy sherry and a ready meal.

And there were the people she had gone to school with, alone or in couples, their babies, children, affairs, and difficult troubles, they brought in raucous stories of wildfire gossip and regularly peppered the days with a soap opera of confidences and opinions. It was recognised she was good to talk to and it was true she was interested, liking to hear how they were getting on, it was more real than stuff on the tv and besides it made the time on her shifts fly by. She hadn't expected that invite from the guy in the car, Matt. Lots of the locals wondered who he was, he had a bit of an air of mystery about him but was always polite and somehow gentle, despite looking like he wouldn't take shit from anyone.

She was flattered he'd asked her for a coffee. But had he asked her out or was she just someone he wanted to be friends with, sensing her kindness? She didn't know which of those options applied. She wasn't looking for a boyfriend. James's needy demands had confused her sufficiently that when the strange controlling behaviour began, she hadn't recognised it as such. He would ring to arrange a date, desperate to see her then let her down a few minutes before they were due to meet, with any number of fantastical excuses: Sorry but the cat was dying at the vet's, Oh my god the office was on fire, his friend's mum needed taking to A and E with a skewer through her hand, but then he would turn up later unannounced when she was just getting over the disappointment and about to go to bed. She had naively been persuaded to move in with him hoping that things might calm down if they were simply at home together. There had been something infinitely compelling about James that fascinated her at the time, caught as she was in a chemical thrall of physical attraction. Last year she had moved back home feeling foolish and bruised. It had put her off getting close to anyone since. But Matt was cute, and she had instantly liked him when he first come into the shop a few months ago. She'd hadn't hesitated to say she'd meet him. Now one of her old school friends came flying in, Belle's mind snapped back to the present as they chatted briefly about an acquaintance who'd had the botox fish lips injection and it had gone wrong. The shop door was shutting behind her when Belle's phone pinged.

You free tomorrow/ Can be round 2pm/ Great- meet outside the shop go for coffee?

She was just texting yes as the lady with the twin toddlers piled frozen chips and nappies onto the counter.

The next day however, when she was starting to get ready after a morning of chores, she wondered why she had so readily agreed.

Unpredictable moments of near panic had been lurking like crocodiles since she managed to distance herself from the twisty bond she'd had with James. Initially she had felt sympathy for him too, he had seemed so unsure of himself then after moving in with him steadily, stealthily, as if by cover of darkness his chaotic timidity had morphed into a fanatical control where he was forever suspecting her of sleeping with every man who had ever stepped foot in the shop. Her kindness was interpreted as lewd and suggestive, her care as a come on to all and sundry. It had left her wondering whether subconsciously she really was unfaithful. If he hadn't been offered a better job in another city, she may not have had the strength to extricate herself.

Serious doubt now occupied her: was it sympathy for Matt, was she a fool set on fixing him, about to complicate her life so soon after simplifying it, what did he actually want from her, maybe the shopwork made her too vulnerable to anyone needy. It swirled around her like a whirlpool when the crocodile takes you under, bubbling into a dark soup until a vision of the vile images James took while she was sleeping came into focus. He had been scathing when she refused to move away with him and had tried blackmailing her with them but soon lost interest when she had held her ground and it was only weeks later she had seen online just how quickly he had found another person to torment. Her phone pings. *See you soon.* She remembered Matt's earnest blushing face, it reminds her they are only going for a coffee at her friend's new café. If he is in any way out of order she couldn't be in a better environment. Public, alcohol free, with other people all around.

'The Tea and Grub Shack' was the new name for what had recently been called Curl up and Dye, a local hairdresser which had taken over from the long-established ironmongers, Palmer and sons. They had gone bust after the big DIY chains came on the market in the out-of-town retail parks.

The new sign was hand painted by the proprietor's partner who was a bit of a handy man himself and might have enjoyed rifling around in the old stock room of Palmer's before the liquidators got hold of it and sold its contents as a job lot at the local auction. Boxes of brass screws, chisels, saws, bits of light fittings, rolls of tape for any eventuality, brushes of all shapes and sizes, dustbins, lightbulbs, door knobs, hinges, batteries and customised string made up a fraction of what you could find in the treasure trove of stock before the bar code and computerised till forced the eternally young Mr Palmer, one of the sons, into his armchair a decade before he was really ready to retire. The bad pun of the short-lived hairdressers wasn't lost on him as he soon lost the will to live without anything to fix, fettle or account for.

The shop had undergone a superficially radical makeover when the weathered floorboards of the old shop were hidden by vino lay and basins and mirrors were plumbed in and fitted to the previously shelved walls. Fruit scented hair products overpowered the faint odour of wood preservative.

The hairdressers had a brief period of prosperity until both Dawn and Findlay who were the top stylists one day decided they were arch enemies and left simultaneously, leaving Marie who they had trained up from a Saturday girl to hold the fort and keep the entire business running for the absent owner who also owned a string of tanning parlours in several nearby towns. It was just a matter of time before the last curls were swept up and Marie had to find another job.

Now the Tea and Grub Shack had taken over the premises to become an on-trend establishment with a state-of-the-art coffee making machine, all day breakfasts and a TGS logo that was printed on locally packaged coffee bean. A vast array of teas was displayed in sweet shop style large glass jars along with home baked biscuits. Scattered artfully upon the newly revealed floorboards was an assortment of mismatched wooden tables with slatted seats that coincidentally had been purchased from the same auction that the ghost of Palmer's stock still haunted.

Belle and Matt pushed open the door which sounded the original bell. It had survived the changes of hands of all the leaseholders, a chiming continuum from past to present. Each tinkle connected one resounding moment to another, one exit to another entrance, the door opening and closing on scenes and episodes in an eternal pulse of possibility.

After all the apprehension about meeting, Belle and Matt found it had been easy to stroll along the treelined street together towards the arcade of shops where the café's newly painted outside tables welcomed passing pedestrians in under an old canvas awning. Gentle ambient music was playing as they went inside to the tinkling of the bell.

Coffee is now the most popular beverage in the world. The ink dark drink keeps people going through all manner of strain and challenge via the gift of its caffeine content. A coffee plant can grow as tall as a tree, blooming with sweet scented white flowers and ripening to produce green beans. When roasted and ground the coffee can be prepared in any number of exotic sounding ways, americano, cappuccino, flat white, espresso, mocha, latte, cortado, all of which involve hot water and the splatter of old grounds into a bin whilst the thump of new are twisted into steely place by a synchronised barista. The resulting bitter liquid can be sweetened with sugar or softened by the froth of steaming milk. It pours into the lips, gullets, and blood streams of all nationalities consuming it everywhere. There is a seemingly endless demand.

Once in the body the coffee turbo charges the adrenal glands sitting on top of the kidneys to create a chemical effect that scores a boost of cortisone thus producing a mirage of seemingly limitless energy from its steaming cup.

They say and it may be true that coffee was discovered by a Yemeni goat who after a day's hard grazing on a hillside was feeling worn down and weary and being a goat, whose entire family are known to eat anything, found the little plant and chewed upon it. The goatherd was uncannily observant and noticed the goat's enhanced energetic state (perhaps its slot pupils had dilated into squares) and reported on it.

Unfortunately, as with any commodity in a ravaged world, the goat's buzzing discovery would result in less favourable outcomes as swathes of rain forest were cut for plantations.

The success of the plant's widespread appeal enriched speculative money makers' businesses with devasting repercussions for local populations forced from their land or into subsistence farming. Coffee by its alluring nature allows the world to keep running from uncomfortable truths.

Where once lush forests prospered, now motorway services' vendors reap the profits of the world-renowned bean in the race to fuel the speed of modern life.

Despite scouring the tanks of our innate energy resources, or perhaps because of it, coffee keeps filling us up with its powerful persuasive potency, cup by cup. Although it was a quiet afternoon in the café. The place wasn't full. There were only a few other people drinking and chatting in quiet murmurs around variously shaped tables. Belle and Matt each ordered a cup and headed towards a table near the window.

'Oh, it's ok in here,' said Matt as they sat down he looking around suspiciously. He had subliminally written off the new cafe as a wanky place that only posers would frequent.

'Yes,' Belle replied, smiling gently, 'the people that run it are friends of mine, which is why I suggested we come here. They've only been open a couple of months.'

'I suppose I shouldn't judge a book by its cover, isn't that what they say?'

Matt isn't sure he hasn't upset Belle, but she bursts out laughing.

'Don't be daft, you can think what you like but it's local and I like it and I've only got a couple of hours before I need to get back to work.'

Matt glanced around the café again, picked up and set down the salt and pepper grinders inspecting them in curious detail then took a sip of his cappuccino uptight and guarded, trying not to lick his lips and hoping the froth hadn't milked his upper lip. How isolated he had become, the other customers sat at ease arms drooping from the back of their chairs, faces laughing or in concentration. He did his best to settle into the warm breeze of Belle's chat, the small boat's sail of him blown along by the simple pleasure of company. With fleeting shame, he remembered fantasising about her, when here now the reality was so much more wholesome and not exactly blemished but imperfect and that was the beauty of it. How many hours, months, days, years had it been since he was able to relax and let down his guard like butter taken out of the fridge and spread on something hot.

Belle for her part kept up an ongoing commentary to maintain a cheery flow of chat and protect any inkling of a quiet place where their individual vulnerabilities lived. After James she wasn't ready to let anyone manipulate her into feeling anything more than she wasn't ready for. Apparently, there are two of them sitting at the table, but other types of eyes would have seen the shadows and influences of multiple people choreographing this encounter, dangling their strings and tugging them to create movement. Belle notices Matt's intense awkwardness, that sips of coffee and room gazing doesn't mask, the stained inner fingers, the posture ready to pounce. Matt senses Belle's underlying wariness, the speed of a bird darting away from any threat with a subtle sensitivity to any nuanced shift. That they are equally matched in their self-protection is something they have in common and so a strange embryonic bond starts to form, they buy a giant cookie from one of the jars and both break their shared half into little pieces that they nibble at like squirrels at an acorn. They notice this and laugh.

Chapter five

Karen arrived amidst the flat lands and indistinct horizons of her brother's neighbourhood dishevelled and stinking of diesel. The porticoed front door was ajar on the latch so she slid surreptitiously into the toilet positioned in the entrance hall where it waited patiently for those who only just made it in time bursting for a wee. Other than that, it appeared to be unused in the multi ensuite household. In the cupboard under the basin, she found some perfumed spray which she wafted cautiously around her skirt so it might hopefully diminish the smell of the fuel whilst not overpowering anyone who stood close by her. Along the lilac carpeted hallway and through the double doors of the living room she could hear the party babbling. Platters of sliced supermarket quiches, and prewashed salad from skin thin cellophane packets adorned the party table next to bowls of cherry tomatoes, cocktail sausages, bread sticks, dips and olives with stabbing sticks that doubled as useful toothpicks. Scarves, lipsticks and smart casual outfits draped the bodies of party goers who were chatting in clumps in the sizeable pale room. Photographic images of light spattered woodlands were spray painted onto frameless canvas. The furniture was scattered with linen cushions whose jaunty colours lifted the monotony of oatmeal walls. Bottles of chardonnay, prosecco and sparkling water glittered next to shiny cans of beer on a drinks table adjacent to the food where wine and bubbly glasses stood upended on napkins waiting to be overturned. Bowls of crisps and nuts were arranged on a family of small tables strategically placed by sofas and chairs. Perhaps thirty people were in the room.

'You didn't!' shouted a woman in shimmering sequins, a gargoyle grimace emerging through thick pan foundation. The red-faced man next to her was shaking with laughter, a fine spray of pastry crumbs recounting a tale of misdemeanour in the workplace.

Down on the taupe velour sofa a suave looking grey-haired gent with shiny loafers and a paisley cravat angled his gooey eyes towards a woman who, looking back at him wistfully batted her heavily mascaraed lashes. With all their powers of self-control they seemed to be resisting a mighty clinch while their eyes roved lustily, lips pursing suggestively.

Karen was still in shock from the petrol forecourt incidence. She sipped a glass of sparkly wine and stood taking in the details of her brother's guests. It was at least 10 years since she had been here, perhaps even at the party for the turning of the previous decade.

The house was modern, built at the end of a small close of similar houses each with individual quirks requested of the builders for extra thousands, a unique garage or novel bay window. Patio doors onto a balcony with mock Tudor battening distinguished one from another with Grecian columned influences. Her brother Jeff and wife Nina had helped design the particularities of their house. At the time Karen had been so bored by these bourgeois details she would read a book while he described the minutiae during the occasional phone calls they had shared.

Now she felt the curious interest of an anthropologist as she settled into the underfloor warmth of this human zoo. She could smell that her woollen skirt was giving off the faintly damp smell of cottage and pump, a mould spore petrochemical mix infusing the arid air.

Her brother caught sight of her and waved an exaggerated semaphore gesture of cliff top to beach proportion then waded cheerfully over. Karen knew the brow wrinkles meant he must be straining to be jovial.

'How are you doing Ka? Good of you to make the journey, thanks.' He was a tall man with eyes that tried not to look too closely and sometimes simply remained shut while he was talking.

'Ah well it isn't every day we turn the big dial and besides you're my closest living relation. Thanks for inviting me.' Karen took a neat sip of wine by way of punctuation.

'But how is my favourite nephew? Surely he's the closest. How's his new job going? I heard he got promoted but had to relocate.'

Why hadn't she prepared for talk of James, it was obvious now that Jeff would ask. Family was everything to him. When they had last talked maybe she had still been in touch with her son, she couldn't exactly remember the sequence or even the details of his software engineering career path.

'I hardly hear from him these days; he thinks I'm a bad and complaining person and that his dad is a saint. To be honest it's probably less painful this way.'

Jeff looked genuinely sad. 'Ouch, poor you. It's never one person to blame is it? You've had a lot of that in your life.' The lines on his brow knitted tighter in sympathy. 'Mum and Dad didn't really understand you; I think they were very frightened by your longing for freedom, of losing you. Maybe I was too and it's possible Jim also. Better to criticise first than be abandoned.'

Karen couldn't reply, a scold's bridle was clamping her speech. Her brother had never spoken before about family dynamics even when as young teenagers they would sneak drinks from their parents' drinks cabinet and get stupidly tipsy. They were the only times she remembered any true connection with him.

'You always seemed to be playing with your life as if nothing really worried you, it was like you were a changeling cut from a different cloth or from another planet.'

They both laughed and she pulled her best 'alien' face, recovering her tongue from its prison. 'Well look at me now, all alone in my quest.'

'Maybe so,' he continued seriously, 'but we've all been through it here too, what with Nina's diagnosis,' he swallowed, 'we've felt alone with our various perspectives. It set me thinking about our earlier life and just how sad our folks were, always pessimistic, if they expressed anything it was the likelihood of failure. I don't want to go that way myself. At least you have blazed your own trail with courage, I'm proud of you for that. It shows spirit and I'm sorry that Jim doesn't appreciate that about you.'

The kindness of this statement left a hard knot of pain blocking up Karen's throat and her eyes struggled to prevent tears. She gritted her facial muscles to control the emotion that was threatening to explode, a hot lava flow erupting through her core. She took a large gulp of the wine and felt the tide recede.

'Thanks,' she managed to say. 'Happy Birthday brother.' Her voice wavered, giving way to the ocean surging in her depths, and she looked directly into his blinking eyes and caught sight there in the slit available to view, perhaps for the first time ever, of something that she recognised as similar.

'I'm sorry about Nina too, how is she?'

'Getting there thanks. In some strange way it's been a good thing for all of us. Helps work out priorities and all that.'

Loaded with all the unexpected intimacy the exchange concluded with a pat on her arm and leaving the complexities undrunk Jeff swallowed from his glass, then turned to play host to a couple in the corner who were standing silently watching the party as if they weren't present there. He smiled as he lifted his head in cheery interest in them. He was the most masterful actor Karen had ever seen. She nodded in respect.

☐

Back in the café the time had evaporated like steam from the espresso machine's wand, and Matt was genuinely surprised when Belle checked her phone and said it was time for her shift in half an hour. They agreed it had been fun and that they'd keep in touch and meet up again but weren't specific where or how, it didn't seem relevant, they could message. They had bonded over rap, drum and bass, clothing, phones and zero hours contracts even as he dodged her tentative questions about his work by being between things at the moment, and he hadn't corrected her when she had assumed the 'things' were some kind of trade. He'd once helped out a mate with some carpentry now and then so now alluded to it confirming her assumption by casual reference to timber framing as he fingered the wooden surface of the table appraisingly. Less lie than self-defence he figured it was way too early to trust to truth. The money he made from doing the deliveries was far more than he'd ever made doing any other job, but it wasn't so easy to dodge the sickening lurch of realisation that he was now trapped in it, and it would not be easy to stop. Although he only dealt with one contact directly, the network depended on him carrying out his part quietly and efficiently. Notorious reputation encircled the boss at the top of the tree, the leaves of which glittered with all manner of ill-gotten gains. The little twig he was in the organisation had once felt proud to be involved with somebody whose power overrode the laws of a hypocritical land of haves and have nots as he looked down at them from his lofty branch. Matt had felt insignificant but protected being in its shade. It hadn't fully occurred to him that the boss owned the tree and could prune, pollard or fell it as and if he chose. It was his. As were those who worked for him. Indentured foliage.

He had been pleased to have successfully drawn Belle away from the subject by telling her about the kung fu class. The less she knew the better. But it had been good to hit on something he could be honestly enthusiastic about. He insisted that he stayed on to settle the bill after they said goodbye, each nonchalantly avoiding any physical contact.

His phone had pinged just after she left.

Tomorrow, 11am, same location.

The message shocked any sense of comforting warmth from him with the suddenness of a quilt pulled off a sleeping body. The reality was an unwelcome trespasser into his fantasy cocoon and dread reminded him that Belle would not want a lot to do with him if she knew how he made his money. A chasm split the ground between his current reality and any potentially different happy future. The cup of coffee dream was impossible, a dull thud on a waking heart. His lies tasted bad in his mouth. It had only been one afternoon in a café but disappointed he pulled down hard edged shutters to create a compromised cell that both protected and imprisoned him. Tomorrow would be fine, it was business as usual. The sweetness of the afternoon was now sour, so what.

He arrived a few minutes early to the place of the delivery. Today, because it was a return visit, and he had some unhappy time to spare he thought he'd explore this nowhere place by stretching his legs and walking up the lane a way. Under the gun metal sky with the chirrup of birds' chatter and the rustlings in the hedge he investigated beyond the layby where a gap in the hedge lead to a partially obscured gate. This he had not expected. There was not a house in sight but looking over the rough hawthorn hedge he could see a few steps and another hedge which distinctly looked like it surrounded a garden. If he was at all familiar with plant life, he would recognise it as privet. Who the hell would live out here he was thinking when he heard a woman's sing song voice calling to an animal by its tone. Moments later, the other car drew up, so he jogged back the few metres to meet it, and exchange the package for the envelope, getting promptly back into his driving seat and accelerating away.

It took him a few calming breaths, the other human had been very close by, close enough for him to hear her voice distinctly enough to hear the pet's name, it was a near miss and as soon as he got the chance he pulled over and texted his contact.

The location is not safe-someone living there/ Who the hell lives in the middle of nowhere? you been smoking that wacky baccy boy? And a crying laughing emoji face. *Any other probs, give us a shout!*

'Fuck you then,' Matt thumps the steering wheel with the foot of his palm furious for not being taken seriously, then doubtful about what he has just heard, and fed up with this cloak and dagger stupidity he throws his phone onto the passenger seat where it slips out of sight behind the boxed goods. He'd be happy enough to do the exchange in a crowded café, after all, who is watching a couple of blokes with a non-descript package? Most of the time he feels invisible anyway. It was probably just some half crazed old bird up there. What did he care.

Karen hadn't registered the cars or any footsteps as she called in the cats for their food. She had only just returned from her brother's after spending the night in a travel lodge where she'd hardly slept but had avoided a late-night drive home after having more than a few drinks.

In the end the party was fun, they had even put on some music and danced to Motown and Stevie Wonder, suave guy and eyelash woman snogging on the patio and Karen surprising herself by feeling glad for them and their bit of passion. You have to get it where you can. A couple who had known her brother since his first job were intrigued to meet his mystery sister. He's a dark horse they whispered conspiratorially; we wondered if he was into some kind of manufacturing espionage when he first joined the firm. Suit, tie and notebook, you know, too good to be true. Never missed a day. Goody two shoes we called him. But underneath it, a heart of gold, a proper diamond when we had our trouble. Here the woman of the pair had cast her glazing eyes downward and took in a trembling breath you don't know who your real friends are until you need them. Karen didn't know whether to ask what had happened, they seemed to want her to, but there was somehow never enough time to interrupt the flow of wine fuelled appreciation, a proper gent he was, came to the hospital and all, we wouldn't have managed without him, sent a card, drove us to appointment's he couldn't do enough.

Jeff and Nina whisked her away just as it seemed they were about to divulge the full facts of their tragedy. You really don't want to know; her brother had said reassuringly. The three of them had laughed at a joke that had no punch line but that relocated her brother to a warmer place in her understanding.

She had ended up talking with a dance teacher who encouraged her to put down her drink and sway along with songs that spun her body on a carousel of known and distant notes riding on the backs of undulating memory horses. And so the party had wound down until her brother had encircled her with a hug and a keep in touch wave as she left in the communal taxi booked for the non-local overnighters.

She had fallen asleep happily but woken soon after in the unfamiliar night reliving the involuntary thing that had animated her hands at the petrol station, it appeared to be imbued with intangible meaning that was tantalisingly familiar but as ancient as cuneiform. An uncomfortable sensation throbbed nervously repeating the invocation she had summoned and in the darkness of the blandly uniform hotel room she admitted to herself that she had issued a curse. It carried responsibility. Perhaps the most perplexing aspect was the apparently automatic nature of it: if she couldn't honestly recognise and take responsibility for that old and familiar something that had worked through her body, what hope was there for her?

On the back of that sleepless thought was another: that she did indeed want to hope and for that to take hold something would have to expand her vision.

Chapter six

Matt missed the kung fu class. Thumping the steering wheel at regular intervals, the stop of a red light, a dawdling driver, a small queue, his irritation had pumped up like a balloon as he drove. Arriving home in in a foul mood he had rolled a spliff tripping over resolves with the satisfying clatter of a tin can on the pavement.

He didn't want to think about any of it. Neither the job nor the prospect that he could possibly free himself from the rutted routine. Although he was hungry, he denied himself the grounding of a meal and instead rationed to a bowl of cereal and tuna from the can, finished off the milk that would have done for the morning.

There had been his mum's funeral, then unfamiliar strangers had taken him and set boundaries and conditions over which he had no control since there was no longer a bond of mutual loving. He hadn't been able to change that, he didn't have the blueprint to make changes now. Maybe it was easiest not to try instead of failing, which would only prove what he'd suspected all along: that he was wasn't worthy of anything good happening. God had already proved that. He rolled another one and took what solace there was in the strange mix of heavy and insubstantial that the weed induced in him. He'd been thinking of texting Belle and suggesting they go out one evening but didn't want to appear too keen as that might put her off meeting up again and besides, she hadn't contacted him either so why should he do all the running? If she wanted to meet again, she too could press those buttons. He was busy persuading himself not to bother when his phone pinged. *Tomorrow same place 1.30pm pick up/ Bad choice/ ?? Says who?/ I told you there's a house there./ Fuck the house./ I'm telling you is all/ Just do it.*

Effing idiots, stupid morons, what the hell, he would pick up whatever shit they wanted him to pick up then he would take a break for a while. Three days in a row. That wasn't usual. They must be stockpiling or something. It would probably go quiet after that anyway. And his money would have mounted up. They could shove their negligence where no sun shone. If they didn't want to listen to his warning them screw them. After that he would give Belle a call. This and the acrid smoke settled him into a plan as the sky turned a deep and inky indigo and the room slid into shadow as he slipped somewhere beneath the dark blanket of it.

☐

Belle was working a double shift late into the evening. It had been a quiet afternoon and she was aware of a let-down disappointment, a deflation of buoyancy after the meet up with Matt. Before it was even properly tied up the new connection had been severed from its mooring by that no news feeling after a job interview. She hadn't thought she would be bothered but like a dog with fleas, rejection scratches old sores.

A quiet fragile child part of her had responded to him, had reached out her hand and although it was touched in response it was not held, but left hanging in an unknown space and she'd had enough of that. Self-protection was now non-negotiable. She needed men friends who were kind and caring, not needy and at the same time complicated, who left you guessing. As quickly as a stop frame sequence of a bud into flower, criticism blossomed into decisive opinion: awkward blushing wasn't sweet, it was pathetic, dog like attention wasn't a promise of loyalty, it was the sign of dependency. Matt's initial reaction to her friend's café had been judgmental. She would now judge him. She had wished him to have sent a quick message, he'd invited her after all, to establish a foundation upon which to build a friendship instead, without that she felt a used fool. Each brick of defence constructed a high wall from the vantage point of which she could view Matt as simply too much of a project. The door of the shop opened, and her dad's mate came in looking for a packet of tobacco and a mars bar. She slipped down off the wall to serve him.

☐

Matt spent a leisurely morning clearing his head with coffee and a shower. He'd adopted the cold shower routine at the end of the steamy hot blast. He liked the ice man he was a bit of a crazy geezer. Water had always been his friend; a shower or swim could reset him. As hot as possible for the soap then lather and scrub away at the relentless sense of contamination that he often felt. Rinsing it down the plughole. Then the onslaught of the cold water brought a tingling cleansing that was both shudderingly unwelcome yet curiously desirable as the magnetism of molecules rearranged under the closing of the skin. Every day a new day, he tried to whistle to repel the invasion of a vague shame. It was now three days since meeting Belle and despite himself he couldn't help checking his phone to see if she had messaged him.

His razored hair had been short for as long as he could remember, he had sought the sparse clarity. But nothing was clear despite the shower and the clean clothes: a non-descript uniform of jeans, t-shirt and padded jacket. He'd worn a dark red shirt when they had gone out. It had hardly even been a date, why was he even thinking about it like that. A tinge of vulnerability had fluttered elusively around her, it had caught his eye momentarily darting in and out of focus. It had given him hope. Sure, she was sweet and friendly and super easy going but the flash of something wistful and gentle that hadn't been cared for reminded him of his mum and how she too had had a streak of sadness that a lack of protection created. Some girls he'd known just seemed tough, but Belle was like a deer, resilient and powerful enough to jump a fence gracefully but preferring the shelter of the forest. She had let him see her without a big front and that was what had been the most interesting. The honesty of it. And that's what he was ashamed of, he wasn't honest. He couldn't be honest. So, he wouldn't call her.

He picked up keys, phone and jacket and closed the door of his flat, shoulders squared to the world. It would be ok. He could go to the kung fu class again. All was not lost. He would give up smoking. He was sick of feeling all this stuff. He was glad to be working now.

Clicking the door of his car open, he drew himself in, gathering together in an act of will learned from the days after his mum. It was the simple necessity of taking the step from one startling void into the next.

By now the journey had become so familiar he had more time to take in the scenery. Tracings of bare limbs angled from trees mourning their lost leaves. Branches scratched the sky above a hedge line that encased the lanes. The roads were crumbling with water collecting asphalt along with it as it ran. Crater like potholes pockmarked the tarmac's surface, and blocked drains spewed muddy rivulets sprinkled with twigs and fallen leaves. A tractor, spikes raised above its cab, was carrying a cylinder of hay speared as if by a medieval jouster. Matt's car was fortunately much lower slung or else he too might have been impaled. Reversing back into a passing place he sighed as the tractor huge wheels spattered mud as it passed. Who would choose to live out here he wondered glancing at the young man in the cab who lifted a lazy finger in casual acknowledgement of his manoeuvre.

Orange lit digits showed 13.15.

Damn, he was way too early. There was nowhere to go to idle away the next fifteen minutes. He felt suddenly conspicuous, to be sitting there uncomfortably waiting for nothing in his shiny blue car. Hopefully the mud would now be something of a disguise. He didn't want to risk driving around, the lanes were a warren, and he wouldn't want to be late that would be worse, so he pulled in to wait, head down as if consulting a map.

She was just coming out of the gate. An older woman, he had no idea how old, anyone over 40 was indeterminate to him. He had lost the privilege of watching a parent age to be able to judge such a thing. She was now walking towards the car. She was waving a pleasant greeting. He felt as skewered as if the tractor's prongs had got him.

In response to her wave, he pressed the button to wind down the window.

'Hi, are you lost?' Her voice was velvety, lacking guile.

'No, I'm just waiting for a friend,' why had he said that? Idiot…

'Oh,' she said quizzically a mild arch of an eyebrow. 'The carpark is up there if you want to get out onto the hill, this is just a passing place.'

'Ah right, we did the what3words thing. I'm sorry I didn't realise.'

'It's not a problem to me love, you wait for your friend here if you like, it's just if a couple of vehicles were to meet, they'd want the space to pass. I don't give a monkey's. Have you come far? Although it's a beautiful place we don't get many people out here.'

He gave the name of a nearby town and remarked on the remoteness of it all.

'Yes,' she said as if she knew him, 'it's away from all the mad bastards who want to get one over you,' then laughed.

He laughed in response. 'I was wondering who would choose a place like this to live in.'

'You'd be surprised, people with things to forget or hide from, the wanting to get away from it all and grow their own food crowd, farmers of course or simply the lure of the beauty of the place catches you and snares you in its trap.' Her hands snapped like a crocodile's mouth. She smiled. Her face was attractive, with sharp almost animal like eyes and a wild crop of auburn hair spattered with lighter silver.

'But don't you get lonely out here?' He surprised himself with the question.

'Sometimes I do, but no lonelier than in the town.' She held out her hand through the window.

'Karen,' she said, 'pleased to meet you.'

He took her hand at the awkward angle the driver's seat allowed, wishing he could get out but spotting the vehicle he was waiting for approaching in the rear-view mirror

'Matt,' he said. 'Ah, here comes my friend, I'll just let him know to meet me up at the carpark.'

He picked up his phone and texted swiftly.

'Nice to meet you too.'

The touch of a friendly hand was warm.

'If you fancy a cuppa after your walk, you're welcome, you can see my cottage from up there, I'll be back in ten minutes or so, just popping to the letterbox.'

Matt didn't know what to say in return, instead he started the ignition, smiled, and indicated to pull out driving further up the hill, the other car behind. Karen stood back into the hedge to let them pass. At the next layby they stopped to exchange the package.

'Who was that?'

'Some local,' Matt said. 'I think she's cool but in future we'll have to sort out somewhere else to meet.' The other was impassive. He was driving empty handed now so it would be Matt who copped it if anyone had clocked them. Bitterness came up to the boil.

Discussion over, the other car drove away and Matt followed slowly. A couple of hundred yards further up the lane was the gateway to the common and a little car park. He pulled in heart hammering, appraising the package he'd tossed onto the passenger seat.

Various scenarios ran in his mind. He was a security guard scanning multiple screens of surveillance cameras.

The woman had seen him, spoken to him, he'd given her his name and if she had been suspicious, she could have noted his reg plate number and the other car's. He watched the effects of these implications descend on his mind like logical guillotines.

Simultaneously he heard a settling voice dispelling suspicion and reassuring him that she had simply been kind and friendly and that he had in fact liked her instantly and would have enjoyed talking more, she had seemed inviting somehow not in a pervy sexual way but dare he even admit it to himself, sort of warm and motherly.

He was staring absentmindedly at the package as it registered that when he did these jobs, he was always time restricted, needing to finish the assignments within a tidy window that was wordlessly expected of him.

The dilemma arose: he had told the woman he was meeting to go for a walk, or more correctly she had assumed this. If he didn't hang around a while wouldn't that arouse any suspicion even further if she lived in sight of the car park? And did it even matter he was so sick of it all.

Usually very efficient he was now in a quandary. He had just cause to prolong his time there on the hill neutralising any potential suspicion. He had done his bit alerting them to the danger of witnesses and they'd taken no notice. He could explain that he was simply making sure he covered his tracks. He would call by for that cuppa and demonstrate the truth of his explanation to the woman then they would have to arrange a new and fresh location for the next consignment. Venues were frequently changed anyway to keep things fresh and untraceable. This place was no exception. That decided he was out of the car and clicking the fob to lock the doors after stashing the package safely in the boot. There wasn't another soul around. He breathed in and tried to relax as he opened the gate and followed the footpath sign up and onto the common. A cool breeze followed him.

Karen had posted her letter. You couldn't beat a hard copy even if it somehow meant responsibility for the loss of biodiversity through single paper use. She resisted much of the online world: it made her feel as if she was living in the wrong era talked to by robots and inputting numbers or saying yes and no instead of a conversation. It only increased her sense of separateness whilst silent money was made from her details and algorithms predicted what she would like to do next.

Besides, her internet connection was so appalling that in the time it took to write something and put it in an envelope, walk to the post box and back she could have been tearing her hair out in front of incessantly revolving screen circles trying to reconnect her. It was these tedious and soul-destroying repetitions that seemed like a metaphor for her life. Endlessly attempting to connect.

Jim who was a techy wizard, used to call her a tedious dinosaur when he was still talking to her. Which she tried to feel was a friendly insult and conjured the fluffy stegosaurus soft toy of his infancy but knew deep down that it was intended to be as critical as possible and typified her as the incalcitrant cow his dad had been unfortunate enough to co-parent with. Whenever she thought of her son, she had to be careful to change the subject. Switch channels, choose otherwise.

What exactly had the lad in the car been up to, there was something unusual about it. The car behind had not seemed like it contained any friend of his, the man was years older and nasty looking.

Karen regretted blurting out that stupid invitation to come and have a cup of tea. What had she been thinking, was she desperate for company at any price? Yet there had been something genuinely appealing about him. It's not every day that you have an instant click with a passing stranger. What was that saying? You meet for a reason or a season…. Simply put, they had taken an instant shine to each other, she could have been his mother. Besides what's wrong with the world, she thought, when you can't even extend a simple hand of friendship to a stranger. She saw that stranger now, walking down her garden path. Before he had seen her, she went to the front door and opened it in greeting.

'Good' she said, 'you decided to risk it, the kettle's just boiled.'

'Thanks,' he replied, stepping over the threshold.

'So,' she said, once the clatter of mugs and the splashing of tea pouring was over, 'this is unusual.' They were sat in the living room, Matt trying not to stare at the details of her belongings and Karen smiling a little too eagerly. Luckily a sleek black cat strolled through the space between them, collecting any friction onto his fur which he then settled down to lick clean.

'Do you live here on your own?' he asked realising as soon as the words were out of his mouth how potentially sinister they might sound but she laughed easily, unbothered by any inference of threat.

'No, it's just me and the cats and occasional rodents. Oh, and an odd slug. And if you count mould spores as living beings then there are millions of us. And how about you are you together with anyone?'

He blushed uncontrollably at the question, even though it was a simple response to his, feeling a curious heat of shame at just how alone he was in the world and how long it had been since anyone had been interested to enquire.

Talking to Belle he had been equally shy of those sorts of direct questions and none of his loosely called mates would have the kind of conversation beyond where they were going and what they were going to do on their occasional nights out.

Karen noticed his reaction.

'I'm sorry I didn't mean to be nosy. It's just I have a son about your age and I don't have much to do with him anymore. I've sort of forgotten about those out of bounds questions.'

Far from easing his discomfort Karen's sympathetic understanding triggered the formation of a lump in Matt's throat which, to his horror swelled as if all the loss and self-defensive strategies he had adopted throughout his life were threatening to gather and be vomited out in a tidal wave.

He looked down towards the worn rug whose threads were exposed like a hungry child's ribs,

'My mum died when I was a boy and I never knew my dad and so I haven't really got a family and no, not a girlfriend, except…'

His voice trailed off as he thought about how much he would like to say that he was going out with someone who made him feel like he belonged somewhere, somebody who he cared about and who cared about him in return. Reaching out to Belle had started inching open that truth in him and now this total stranger was crowbarring the door.

Karen reached out her hand and gently stroked his. 'I know what it's like to have a broken heart, love, I didn't want to pry but I can recognise pain and loneliness.' They sat, both struggling to control tears, exerting useless energy to perpetuate a stoic myth.

'Goodness me, this meeting of ours has become unexpectedly deep all of a sudden.' Karen's voice when she spoke was firmly back in control.

He was grateful for her honesty and for steering them away from the unexpectedly painful intensity. 'Yes. I've got to go now but I have really liked meeting you.' He wanted her to know how much.

'Me too.' She replied simply, 'come by again and we can be better prepared to tell our stories. You probably will think I'm a mad old bat, but I reckon we have known each other before. Cheesy as that might sound you are familiar to me.'

'I don't really know what you mean,' he replied regaining some of his composure as he stood to leave. 'But I'd like to know more. I spent a long time watching my Mum die and wondering where she went. It's hard to know what life is supposed to be about.'

Karen stood up too and put her arms around him in a hug. He awkwardly patted her back. The tender warmth of encircling arms softened a millimetre of hardened crust, of parched and arid ground.

'Thanks,' he said embarrassed by the intimacy.

'Thank you.' She replied, 'see you again sometime.'

It was gathering dark as he walked to the car, the sky a grey shawl wrapping itself around the shoulders of the earth. The breeze had died down.

Ah! So much facilitated by the simple offer of a cup of tea. Char, chai, Tcha. Tea. Such generous currency. The small shrubby tree camellia sinensis grows bountiful leaves that provide all manner of excuses to share a moment. Tea's appeal is universal. Will you take a cup, the kettle's on, who'll be mother, have a nice cuppa and a biscuit. Wherever you go in certain small northern islands you'll likely be offered a cup of the quintessential beverage.

Initially, before its greater popularity in Britain, when tea was just quietly growing away in China, someone had introduced it into elite medical and scientific circles as a highly medicinal drink. Then with growing fame drinking tea became fashionable and wealthy aristocratic ladies who wanted to show off took to taking a cup with friends in the afternoon as a social pick me up, their little fingers held aloft as if unsure where to tuck themselves. Finest porcelain cups were chinked dangerously vulnerable into saucers by the remaining digits.

Later merchants and trading companies manipulated imports to monopolise business interests and promote exports that were colonial fuel. Tea's story was a marketing success while indentured labourers were enslaved on tea plantations.

Tea as a gasping life saver was achieved by boiling water and diminishing mortality rates, cholera and typhoid couldn't survive the heat of the tea making process.

The rusty brown drink, though slow to take off due to costs and taxes soon enough would fuel British society's workforce. With milk and sugar added tea provided the caffeine and calories to survive the gruelling demands of an industrial working day.

Tea enabled women to go unchaperoned into a tearoom and still retain their dignity thanks to its blessing of respectability. In a relatively cold and wet climate a warming hot brew during a tea break or tea party was successfully ritualised with immortal appeal. Drinking tea was adopted as a national pastime. There, poured into the caddies, boxes and pots of nearly every household in the nation, tea became an unmitigated influencer and is still the cause of many an encountas cuppas are fancied up and down the country. Karen and Matt may not have met without it.

Chapter seven

Sean was finding himself increasingly weary, he hadn't felt quite well lately. At the end of a shift where once the many tasks and problem solving thrown up during the ten hours of work had caused him to thrive, he was now knackered. He liked the job and enjoyed being good at it. This was why he'd been promoted. The fact that his reputation as an uncompromising taskmaster or f****** w***** caused him to be despised didn't really bother him. In fact, he felt the taskmaster to be the major shareholder of his personality, and he admired that in himself. His power was enviable.

But now the fatigue was threatening his identity. If he couldn't beat it, then others would overtake him. This was intensely problematic: life was, and always had been one giant ongoing competition. He hadn't been particularly smart at school, but he worked out the game and knew who to be friends with. Willing to put up with a lot of what he supposed would now be called bullying, had in practise taught him the skills to bully, so it had been worth it. His wife and kids submitted to his will because after all he was the man of the house and bought in the money and paid for everything. He had them over a barrel.

From this approach he derived a sense of purpose and security. If accused of abusive behaviour by colleagues and staff, he would wield his power and win, accusing others of a lack of commitment, a failure of motivation, laziness. With these as his reasons he would explain how they were mistaken, and he was correct.

That incident the other day, he'd worked that one well, though he'd had to have a stiff word with the maintenance guy who'd forgotten to reconnect the automatic cut off mechanism. He was proud that he'd saved the company a lot of money in compensation. It would no doubt be reflected in the bonus that was awarded if there were no insurance claims against them.

Nevertheless, he couldn't help associating this feeling of fatigue with that weird moment when what had she said? 'You'll regret this' or something like that. He looked at his watch and pushed himself up to standing. Things wouldn't get done if he didn't make sure they did.

He usually woke at 6am. He liked the quiet potential of the early morning before the others were fighting for the bathroom and bickering over breakfast. It gave him the space to collect himself before the thousands of demands of a working day. He prided himself on his ordered controlled capacity to deal with one thing after another, but those things had to be presented in a linear fashion or else. His family knew this, Cathy, his wife put up with it with sour acceptance, begrudgingly compromising her satisfaction for financial ease. He had little insight into just how many people now actively disliked him and his cold rigidity.

Brutally efficient, he liked to think of himself as a well-oiled machine. That machine, however, was grinding to a halt. An agonising granite lethargy was creeping up on him, all the moving parts were seizing up, short circuiting wiring and when he tried to put his foot down to rev his internal accelerator the cable had snapped, no connective power. His body was such a dull weight when he awoke that even his eyelids needed focused concentration to open.

Yesterday he called in sick, something he had never done before.

Today he has managed to get an appointment with the doctor.

The doctor, a smart woman younger than him by a decade welcomes him into the consulting room waving towards a chair,

'So,' she says in a measured but caring enough way, 'what seems to be the trouble?'

'I thought that was your job to tell me.' To himself he sounded authoritative, might as well let her know who she was dealing with. She stares back, impassive. If she had worked for him, he would have suggested that she took less time quietly looking at him and got on with the job.

'OK, let's start again. Why have you come to see me today?'

He struggles to control a wave of irritation. 'I am unwell, can't you see that? Otherwise, I wouldn't be here. You need to check me out. Tests and things.'

'What sort of unwell? Are you in pain? How long have you been feeling this way?'

Some patients knew all the Latin translations of their self-diagnosed problems, others thought she had x-ray eyes and clairvoyant powers divining what was wrong with them just by their presence. And of course, there were also many who consulted the google guru. She had been working as a GP for four years now and people's expectations never ceased to amaze her, satisfaction was hard won, she could already sense that the system was closing in on her, crushing her idealism like a car in a breakers yard.

This specimen was particularly dense. She takes a calming breath.

'I don't feel well. I had to take a day off. It's not pain exactly I just haven't got any power left in me, it's like I've run out of steam. It's been getting worse over the past 10 days or so.'

The doctor picks up a stethoscope and he visibly relaxes. At last, he thought, she's going to do something.

She listens to his chest front and back, asks him to breathe in and out. Next, she velcroes the blood pressure cuff onto his upper arm, the ripping sound of a thousand hooks and purchases scratch at his hearing as she adjusts it to fit. It tightens on his arm constricting the internal blood vessels in a boa like vice, then just as his ears are pounding fit to burst it releases in anti climax. Now she is sticking a thermometer in his ear, pulling down the skin below his eyes to see the colour of the lower lid. Each procedure diminishes his sense of autonomy, any confidence deflating as rapidly as the released cuff.

He lets it all happen quietly but when the questions start again his impatience flares.

'Look, my appetites ok, I haven't lost any weight, I'm not peeing more or less than usual, and my bowel movements happen as regularly as they ever did. Can you please simply tell me what you think is going on? I feel awful.'

Horrified he hears a note of desperation in his voice.

'Well Mr Lewis. There's nothing in any of these checks that lead me to any firm conclusion. In fact, congratulations, everything looks good and healthy for a man of your age. Blood pressure is fine, chest clear, temperature normal. If this was a medical examination, I'd give you a shining bill of health.' She smiles encouragingly.

'It is a bloody medical examination and basically you haven't found anything wrong with me, so I am starting to suspect you don't know your job very well.' Exploded exasperation spatters out from him, bounces off the consulting room's walls.

'Mr Lewis, I need to remind you of our zero-tolerance policy on abusive language in this practice.' Her smile has disappeared. 'But I am wondering have you been under undue pressure at work of late?'

He blows air out of his cheeks. This is below his belt. Low down and insolent.

Before he has the chance to parry with an observation on her lacking skill set, she continues, fingers tapping her computer's keyboard at impressive speed.

'I'm going to prescribe you these tablets, they are the lowest possible 2mg dose and you can take them up to three times a day. They are what used to be called Valium. I hope they will help you deal with the anxiety and stress you've obviously been under. See how you get on with them and then make an appointment at reception to see me again in about 10 days' time and we'll take it from there.' A brief nod and she turns back towards the screen. He realises that he has been dismissed.

The hall was in darkness as Matt approached. He checked his watch and wondered why nobody seemed to be about with only a couple of minutes before the class was due to begin. Disappointed, he was just turning to walk away when he noticed a slip of paper poking out from the letter box on the door. It was the back of a till receipt with a note scrawled in dying biro with a phone number, Sorry had to cancel at short notice, Gus.

It had been a big enough decision for Matt to return to the class that Gus bothering to leave the little note caused a curious surge of affection. Without hesitating he rang the number, gazing idly at the printed purchase descriptions on the flip side of the note, butter, lettuce, sardines, subtotal £9.37 change from a tenner £0.63 until a croaky voice answered.

'Gus? It's Matt, I came to your class for the first time the other week, I just found the note at the hall. Are you OK?'

'Hey Matt, good to hear from you. I'm ok.' He laughed with a croaky hard-edged rasp. 'Actually, my throat's like a razor and I feel crap. But by next week should be fine if you can make the class then.'

'Sure,' said Matt. 'I'll be there or if not, I'll let you know. Oh, and thanks for letting me know.'

They rang off. Matt felt hope glimmering like light surrounding an ill-fitting door. It poured liquid around the edges of obliterated vision, forming shimmering pools: Gus, the leopard man, Karen the laughing witchy woman on the hill and Belle, with her sweet smile. Good things were happening to him. Why on earth hadn't he even sent Belle a message? He set off on foot in the direction which took him straight past the shop where she worked.

As he pushed open the door, he thought he might not find her there. It was quiet other than a couple of customers grazing like cows among the shelves. An older man was stacking cigarettes and tobacco into the screened off compartment behind the till. The blank packaging with the bold black government health warnings made it difficult to differentiate between brands as he stacked them into place. What a con this was, pretending to care about health whilst turning every other screw to make people feel poorer and more unhappy. Matt knew smoking didn't do you any favours, but he also knew that during his loneliest times he didn't need politicians punishing him for the fact especially when so many of them snorted cocaine in the toilets of the houses of parliament. And he happened to know that for a fact, he had probably handled a package that had ended up there. Belle emerged from the alcohol aisle flattening a cardboard box. They stopped short about 6 feet away from each other, chocolate bars and chewing gum holding the distance between them. Matt watched Belle's naturally open face close like a flower at sunset.

'Oh hi,' she said dropping the folded cardboard and stamping it down with a certain force.

She started to turn away when Matt said simply 'have I offended you? I'm sorry I didn't message; I don't know why I couldn't, but I wish I had.'

She returned his gaze with a cool stare. 'Ah well, never mind. I too could have sent a message but decided against it.' She said this with a barb that she wanted to sting but simultaneously regretted, it seemed to show more interest than she wished to display.

'Right. I did wonder.' He set his face in as non-committal an expression as he could muster. 'No worries. It was nice to meet up anyway.' He shrugged and foolishly picked up a packet of biscuits somehow thinking that it would save his honour if he had a reason for going into the shop other than to see her, just like the loaf that had ended up going mouldy in his breadbin.

The bloke who had been filling the shelves had disappeared, so Belle had to log herself into the till to serve him.

'You say you couldn't send a message, what happened, did you lose your phone?' The edge was sarcastic but at least there was a conversation going on.

'No, it wasn't that, just it was complicated...'

'Oh! Had you forgotten how your phone works?'

He snorted. Almost laughed. 'No, it's just that....'

The other worker returned from out of the stock room and was heading their way, 'I'd rather not talk about it here.'

'Well, there's nowhere else we'll be talking about it.'

'You alright Belle?' said the fellow worker.

'Fine, but would you mind if I quickly took five?'

Once the wooden exchange for the unwanted packet of biscuits was completed with a slam shut of the till drawer, Belle came out from behind the counter and walked down the far aisle of the shop beside the fridges.

'Look Matt, it was just a cup of coffee, but I thought we had made friends and I don't treat my friends with a stone wall of silence.'

'You could have messaged me,' he replied hating the slight whine in his voice.

'Yes, I could have, but given the disaster that was my last boyfriend, I wanted to find out what sort of person you were. And I discovered that.'

He didn't know how to reply. Feeling belligerent he asked what exactly she had discovered.

'I don't know exactly, but something doesn't feel quite straightforward with you. I wasted a lot of time wondering why you didn't simply get in touch and yes, I could have but I thought it was up to you. After all you were the one who invited me. Then it all felt too complicated, and I'm not interested in anything complicated.'

Having spoken she seemed relieved.

'Well, that was good. Now you know there's nothing doing. And I've got to get back to work.'

She almost smiled as she brushed past the packets of pasta and walked off. Matt's grasp on the biscuit packet intensified as he felt their round edges crumbling under the pressure of his fist. It wasn't anything he didn't already know.

◻

Across town in a slightly upmarket neighbourhood a young social worker named Alice was writing a report.

Another child would be looking for a foster home. What were these people on, why have kids if you couldn't recognise a nonce or sober up enough to put the kids to bed. She knew those thoughts were totally unprofessional, that she was getting worn out by the degradation of it all. Wearily she closed the laptop.

Night had fallen, an inky stain seeping onto the street below her first floor flat. She drew the curtains blotting out the dark and clicked on the golden glow of the lamp.

She loved this flat perched as it was above shops, whose only access was through the dark red door between electrical appliances and the new zero-waste place that had only opened a year ago. Once through the flat's front door which locked heavily behind her there was a steep staircase from a windowless hall that led to another lockable front door. Beyond this was her haven. It didn't fully register how closely the double locking doors with their vacuum of hall space resembled the entrance to the prisons in which she sometimes had to carry out interviews.

Alice had made a point of supporting the new shop when it first opened, thinking no one else would, but was surprised to find it becoming a bustling hub with children weighing things on the scales and delighting in pressing the buttons to print out price labels for rice, coffee beans, cereals, spices, nuts, raisins, and more. Playing shop was fun. Adults enjoyed chatting by the jars and containers. Some control was needed to prevent flooding in the sticky section for liquids refills. Wooden shelves held cards by local artists, handmade soaps, and sometimes fresh baked cakes. The enterprising shop owner watched proceedings with hawk eyes and bantered like a market trader, giving the shop an entertaining feeling of security and a spacious sense of theatre where anything might happen. Alice wished she had this woman's sharp clarity and noted when her teenage kids came in for the occasional shift that they too seemed self-assured in a way that she quietly envied. Occasionally on difficult days she avoided going in there because her confidence already low would plummet further. Today had been one such day: arriving home after desperate meetings whose cobweb sticky stories clung on as she typed them up. She decided to run a bath, needing to soothe an agitated sense that the woes of the world were piling up around her, threatening to suffocate, poking at her privilege, submerging her, their never-ending iterations pebbles in her pockets weighted to drown her.

Steam thickened the air in the glow of a tub side candle, her bathroom became a warm wet womb, she slid her body under the liquid balm of safe containment in the tub. Somewhere in the centre of her belly or was it even an actual physiological space, she felt cracked. A subterranean convulsion wracked her with a profound and relentless sorrow. She had willed herself immune to this kind of tectonic shifting. She was a trained professional, she was the one supposed to be in charge, the one to make informed decisions about safeguarding and protection, she was supposed to know best.

Through the crack she glimpsed an innocent little girl who had loved a granny, simply and without question. Granny whose hand she had held through the park as they gazed at red tulips standing to attention and chatted under the pink blossom of cherry, idly tossing crusts to pigeons and ducks by the crap spattered city pond while older kids whizzed by on BMX's and mums pushed buggies and blokes sauntered around on the lookout for action.

During her own early years of school and nursery when her parents were busy working, granny was the haven. Very suddenly she was gone, the central anchor of her life was taken, and in her place a sure threat and the certainty of violence in the world. She had not been allowed to attend the funeral which had been delayed by a post mortem. Her parents, as distraught as she by the violent death, had sent her to spend the day with kind friends. Nobody saw how this dislocation from the traumatic reality would create a further shadow that lingered like a lost ghost in the halls of the child's inner architecture.

Why would they, wrapped up as they were in shock and only a few generations away from when children's silent compliance was expected, 'better for them not to have to deal with it.' Alice had behaved, locked up the fear in an unknown room and chosen child protection as a career, blindly believing that would banish the ghost.

Chapter eight

Twenty-five years earlier

Myra couldn't possibly have known it was going to be her last day. There were no signs as she got up to pee in the early morning that she would never do this again. Yes, the toilet seat was feeling a little further away than it used to but at seventy-eight years old she didn't feel so different inside than she had aged forty. People gave up their seats on the bus, and in the supermarket they asked if she needed help packing her shopping. She still lived only a few streets away from the childhood home where she and her sisters had been born and raised after their parents had arrived in the country. It was a different world now from the one she had grown up in. The bay windowed brick house had been converted into a few flats, had lost the front garden's cherry tree whose May blossom had enchanted her with its fluffy pink snow, the hard stoned fruit a treat for a variety of birds. Now multiple municipal bins, flat numbers painted on them, rested on a specially concreted platform where pigeons pecked, rats slithered, and the fox feasted on black bin liners' innards that spilled over the corpulent sides of the bins' bellies. The downgraded beauty bought a certain sadness. Mostly though, change inspired her innate dynamism as the population and habits of the neighbourhood rose and declined like ancient civilisations, new smells on the breeze, different fashions parading the streets. She was a volunteer at a local school and sometimes covered for one of the charity shops that had been a grocer's business when she was a girl. It kept her up to date, her diary was as busy as ever with various projects. Just occasionally a mundane detail could trigger a sharp pain of missing her dead husband: the demolition of an old building, a traffic rearrangement, the annexing of a green space for flats. Places they had known together changed irrevocably. Cupid had been very kind to them. Myra knew she'd been well loved; her grief was proportionate to the preciousness of her marriage. When you'd been around the block a few times, she would say, mischievous eyes sparkling like faraway stars, you knew enough that there were cycles to the mysterious unfolding of ups and downs, of springs following winters and not to get your knickers in a twist. There can be so much that is phoney and patronising about being good hearted, but kindness and humility and taking a genuine interest in the common welfare of people was the most important currency as far as they both had been concerned. And life had rewarded them with children and the steep learning curve that comes from raising a family. The especial and unexpected jewel was her little granddaughter. Though favouritism was almost forbidden in her world view she couldn't deny the special bond she felt with the little girl. As if they had always known each other. A connection that needed no explanation and provided such solace in her widowhood. From the moment of this little one's birth, they had shared an affinity that defied explanation. Like a pair of knitting needles, together they knotted a mutual blanket from the yarn of their existences. If she had known there would be no goodbye to this little soul mate perhaps that would have been the thing that broke her heart, more so than the apparently senseless and desperate violence that was to be the manner of her downfall.

After breakfast she applied her lipstick in the hall mirror and checked her hair before putting on her winter coat. She didn't say goodbye to the house, the olive-green carpet of the hall and stairs, the kitchen that had cooked thousands of family dinners, the garden with the canes of raspberries, the set of plates flying up the wall, the notes by the phone, the key fobs, the cushions on the sofa, the sideboard with the glass ware, the umbrellas sat at the door. The stuff of a lifetime in a semi-detached neighbourhood. They'd come here from a flat above a shop and it had felt so spacious and affluent. There was no premonition as she closed the front door behind her that she would never return. Mercifully. How could we live with such knowledge, trying desperately to prevent it happening.

No, she simply strode along the road with her navy-blue handbag strung over her shoulder secured at the armpit by her hand. Marching up the street.

Final things are not only in the domain of the dead. They are what is left behind for those that mourn the last time each thing happened. The time they laughed like drains over a stupid mistake. Or when she wore that dusky blue jumper with the lovely neck, and they pretended to be strangers on a packed train. They had winked at each other across the seats, she had snorted, and her neighbour had tutted and then they hadn't dared meet the other's eye for fear of exploding into uncontrollable laughter. The ache in her belly had been the perfect blend of pleasure and pain. Final birthday cards ever signed and sent to best friends and family, looked at afterwards as if they were ghosts, the handwriting jolting a spasm of longing, knowing she would never again be seen opening the door with a smile or rounding a corner with a wave of farewell. When the loving is finished and the quarrels are over, the final curtains flounce to the stage boards. When that finale is caused by another's hands there is a chaotic chasm.

Myra boarded the number 402 bus that would take her to her meeting with ten minutes to spare. The bus was steamy inside from the condensation of the damp bodies sprinkled with January rain. No one could see out through windows spattered with droplets of rain. There was a fuggy friendliness in the atmosphere, a collective shelter for all bought temporary equality to the chugging interior of the bus. She thought of these fellow city dwellers as distant family relatives related by urban challenges. It was perhaps a by-product of understanding the outsider that her life had taught her. Them and us was a construct to have power over the other. Who needs that? It's complicated enough just getting by and keeping the peace. Myra reached her stop and got off the bus, having a bit of spare time she popped into the post office. In luck, no queue. She cashed her pension. She heard the fast footsteps, felt the proximity of someone very close to her back, the sudden pulling backward of the handbag. She yanked it back towards her and the full force of the give it to me momentum unbalanced her as she was thrown by the pendulum effect of back and forth gathering pace toppling her until thwack, no time to cushion the blow with an arm or a bum, just a cranium impacting on paving slab. She heard the footsteps recede, running away like a distant memory that can't quite be caught and as the consciousness poured out from the river of her life, the blood poured out through the newly combed hair to congeal on the slab. Perhaps she looked down on the felled tree of her body, felt the shocked care of the passers-by, the shouts and cushioning of concerned hands. As the cold gathered, seeping in to exchange places with the warm hearted being the infinite moment released the incarnate soul into the big everywhere as invisible stars spiralled in the heavens.

He runs hard, breath burning in frightened lungs, heart pumping with horror, it wasn't what he'd thought would happen, it wasn't what he'd meant to do, it wasn't his fault, why did she have to hang on to the fucking handbag? With lungs bursting, he has to slow down, to slow the adrenalin pumping his system like a jackhammer through concrete. His peripheral vision sees the suburban street, the trees by the kerb stones in slab free squares. His legs cool to walking pace, the bag is bundled beneath his jacket, a false pregnancy. He risks a glance behind him and sees the parked cars, the distant flats, hears the vague thrum of traffic, the whine of sirens, tastes the parched throat of exertion. Thwack, bodies are thrown at him as if from nowhere, grab his arms, tripping his feet, taking him down. A defeated domino.

Myra is dead on arrival to hospital. She'd already gone when the ambulance crew took over from the horrified pedestrians who had encircled and made her as comfortable as they could, covering her in coats, making a pillow with their jumpers. They had simply happened to be there at a precise moment that would define the rest of their lives with the experience. They wouldn't forget.

When the police arrive, he is cuffed red-handed. Then bundled into the back of the police van and driven to the cells in the station. Coming down moment by moment he briefly thinks of the girlfriend he'd abandoned when she had told him she was pregnant, the little boy he'd never known as a son. He didn't usually give them a second thought. He may never think of them again as there are now the more pressing issues of threats and blows, the cell, the others in it, the loss of freedom. Allowed a phone call, he has rung his dad. There is a silence when he picks up. He was already exasperated, there had been so much trouble lately, as a parent he doesn't understand where he has gone wrong with this son for whom he had done his best. He doesn't want to be held responsible. There was no prospect of bail, what does he think he could do? It seems the simplest and least painful option for the rest of the family to cut all ties and try to avoid the shame of having a murderer as one of their own. He knows it was the drugs that have destroyed him, it breaks his heart to think of his own little lad taking a life, taken so low. He's warned him, repeatedly. But he's not a lad anymore, he has become dishonest and mean young man, preying on the weak and vulnerable. Who did he think he was dragging them all into the shit with him? Of course, it would be all over the local papers. It had even hit the national news but only because for that day there hadn't been anything worse to report. Luckily, they hadn't used his name yet. 'Look son, I'm sorry, I really am but I can't help you this time. This time you're on your own, you're going to have to face it, try and clean up your act.'

They finish the call. Cold spreads through him, a type of death infiltrates his defencelessness. Resigned, he squares his shoulders and is led back to the cell as if to the gallows.

Time crawled like lice on his skin but gradually a routine etched its stern edicts into his days. Lights out, get up, eat, work, eat, exercise, gain small privileges, lose others, Lights out. Until suddenly the waiting was over, a court convened, a sentence handed down and here he was starting his actual payback time. A portion of a lifetime for a life. He was sentenced for manslaughter, got seven years, could be out in five. Whatever gentleness he had once known, gentleness which had vanished as soon as he lost the chubby cheeks of early childhood was now totally absent from the hard-edged face that had to decide to attack before being attacked and be more vicious than the next fucker. He was known and feared for his humourless sneer. Shadow feeds on shadow and dark and sticky places build up like nauseating bile where entities of vile cruelty, victimisation and despair hang heavy in the corners of the institution. A general malevolence dripped from the overcrowded prison walls. There were three of them in his cell. He was the youngest in years but physically could threaten his way into the best bunk. The older less fit men didn't want to provoke the smouldering rage in that sneer, he was a mean asshole. The limits of his cell completed his degradation, there was no room for growth, nothing to expand upon once the other guys were subdued. He only saw diminishment. And so, it happened: before long he found his place in the wider scheme of things outside the cell. He soon learned who to listen to, who to obey, who to stamp on, who to ignore and how to pay for whatever it was he wanted to take the edge off the daily grind of her majesty's service. It was only a matter of time before the lethal gear found its way into his veins and he was found stone cold, still on his bunk, a ball of vomit blocking his throat. The other guys had been snoring as he choked, they explained. There was little reason for it to have been otherwise. Alone with their small son Matt's mum didn't know his life had ended, never got to hear that his economy funeral had taken place discreetly and with only immediate family members who could bear to witness it. She had read all about his conviction in the papers and had scrupulously erased any connection to her little son to save him the knowledge of it. His family didn't know anything about a child or a girlfriend. They had never been told. Maybe there might not have been the need to protect Matt from the possible reappearance of his father. But it had felt safer to keep it all quiet.

☐

The opium poppy has a most beautiful flower. Delicately fragile petals of fine tissue paper quality surround a dark centre where the stamen flutter outwards, feeling into the vibes of the world. At the base of the flower the stem starts to swell until the seed head forms a magnificent orb with openings all around its crown. In time this orb will scatter out millions of tiny poppy seeds in a fountain of abundant reproduction.

If when the seed heads are still green, you were to slit them from crown to base an oozing substance appears. This is the beginnings of the opium/morphine/heroin that will end up in smoke, or into the veins of people searching relief from pain they sometimes do not even realise they feel or in search of dreams that the harsh world does not afford. Poppies, those emblems of war, poppies, those bringers of peace, poppies, the mess of addiction, the junk in the junkie, the fields laid waste, the violence of demand. They call her the grey lady, great melancholic sorrow surrounds her, as surrounds all that which is gravely manipulated where dreams lie in tatters. In the syringe drivers of the dying whose lives are twisted by the agonies of disease, she is said to ease the passage from disappearing life.

In the pipes of the dreamer, she banishes sensations of pain and promises the greatest equanimity in existence. Small wonder she is sought out time and again, then again and again until the dream swallows itself whole to devour the seeker in desperation. In the needles of the lost she delivers oblivion when responsibility has resigned, and self-respect is contaminated. Lie still and float in suspended gravity. Bliss until the next fix is needed, at any expense. In the smoke of the decadent, she is the dragon chased for the treasure horded in her innermost being. Dragons, though potentially benevolent are not ultimately in service to those who choose to abdicate their human mission.

With a smile on her beautiful face, the grey lady slips through the needle and enters the blood stream dissolving feelings and vaporising resistance. A little poison now and then, too much and it will be the premature end of your journey, the need to vomit battles with the soporific need to lie back. The ghost gives up.

There's a line that can't be crossed without everything that was once experienced becoming irrevocably reallocated. The line separates this physical plane from that which lies beyond. The live breathing body dissects the line and rots with the removal of the animating force. The death mask is still. There is only absence. The intoxicated spirit may however not fully realise its own demise, lost as it was in life, it may yet remain stuck in the prison of another realm.

Myra's children would all say they have got over her death. They don't give the manner of it any further thought; it was a long time ago; the violence was born of addiction, but life must move on. We cannot mourn forever they had said.

Although a small child on the day of Myra's death her granddaughter Alice can remember the smell of her granny's house, it lingers homoeopathically on the clothes she inherited after all the tidying up, when the business of death had been executed.

Chapter nine

Matt was summoned to a pub in the nearby big city. It was said that Queen Elisabeth the first had overnighted there back in the day when her royal travelling party needed sustenance and a place to rest weary bones after hours in rickety carriages and saddles on horses' backs. Matt reckoned it was one of those stories that grimy hotels claim as their heritage: the Beatles stayed here on their first tour of Leicestershire, or Lulu slept in this bed on her debut night in Plymouth. These claims on historicity bestowed their own version of blue plaque favours upon establishments never mind the veracity. Whatever the truth of the story of this pub, it was indeed a mighty old building. Massive oak timbered beams scarred with worm and nailed holes latticed the ceiling while floors that sloped like a vessel at sea slid away to wattle and daubed walls. It was marooned in an island memory of its age, surrounded by roads and younger buildings, some nobly Victorian, others brutally 1970's.

His summoners were three older men who sat casually at a table by the giant fireplace, which was as big as a walk-in wardrobe and unlit at lunchtime. They were cradling their drinks and checking their phones. He had only met one of them before and felt a respectful nervousness that bordered on potential dread, though this was beyond admitting, because then it would show somewhere, be read on his face or in his gestures so he simply denied feeling it. He was clever like that or perhaps more accurately, well-practised.

'Ah Matt,' said the man he knew as Ray, 'come and sit down. Drink?'

'I'll have a coffee please, don't drink on duty.'

If he had hoped to break the ice the freezer door stayed firmly shut. The elder of the other two men took a slow sip of what looked like whiskey and eyed him coldly.

'Do you know why you're here?' he was surprisingly well spoken.

'No sir, I do not,' the respect had a very slight thawing effect.

'Well, there's a couple of things to straighten out here. The first is that when you work for us, you keep our time and not your own…The other day your late delivery caused all sorts of trouble further down the line.'

'With all respect,' Matt interrupted, 'I can explain my reasons for the timing on that day. I had warned my contact that the chosen location was compromised, and nobody took any notice so when the lady who lives up there saw us, I thought it best to follow through with the story I had told her by way of explaining our presence there.'

The man held up a single finger in warning.

'There's a couple of things here I would disagree with Matt,' he pronounced his name with venomous precision. 'The first is that I didn't ask for an explanation and the other is I can't stand it when people pass the buck. Do you understand me?'

Matt had the idea that this man may well have been trained in the army, he decided to treat him as such. 'Yes sir.'

'So, when we book you to courier some goods you deliver them at the expected time, not some DPD style equivalent. Am I clear? We have customers needing precision timing. You are merely a component in a much larger working machine, a very tiny component at that.'

'Heard and understood,' said Matt with as much servility he could manage.

He couldn't help but wonder if the spirit of the late Queen herself had entered the man, so highly did he appear to rank himself. Assuming himself duly reprimanded he stood and said, 'I'm sorry it won't happen again.'

'We're not done here yet,' said Ray quietly. Matt sat back down. As if a light switched on the man assumed a much friendlier posture and tone.

'Your efficiency in all other regards has been noticed however, and we have a very rare opening for which we are considering you.' The final word of this

80

sentence threw a forceful punch that hit Matt's solar plexus. 'Oh,' he replied, trying to squash the rising panic in his chest and appear as if he was somehow flattered. 'We'd like you to help us expand operations within your area of expertise. Take on a bigger role so to speak, use the efficiency you have always shown and put it to greater use, realise your potential.' Matt may not have known these men personally, but he did know what they were capable of when they didn't get what they wanted and how. 'Thank you for considering me, I'm flattered' he replied humbly and could tell with relief that he had struck the right chord as the main man relaxed the grip on his tumbler and tapped it gently causing the glass to ring with a tinkle. 'This is of course a preliminary meeting, just a beginning. They are various strands and threads that need to fall into place before any definite plans or contingencies happen, expansion always needs caution. I trust you can keep this to yourself.'

'There's no one I would share it with. But can I ask what it would entail and what it might be worth to me?' Matt calculated that he needed to show a bit of self-interest as well as the humility. It worked.

'If I say international expansion, that should give you an inkling.' The man smiled if you could call the sharp-eyed grimace a true smile. 'Money would increase.'

'And if it didn't feel like the right opportunity for me at this moment in time?'

'There would not be another opportunity, or moment,' he replied with a cold return to ice, the threat lying frozen between them. After a few cursory farewells Matt was then dismissed, the men had other business to discuss. He was instructed to make contact by the end of the week. Leaving the pub, throat tight, ribcage locked, Matt wanted to scream. 'Fuck, fuck, fuck, fuck, fuck, fuck, fuck, fucking bastards,' he ranted as he walked at a pace to where his car was parked. Often in the past it had helped him deal with all sorts of setbacks to swear forcefully. He had never understood why it was considered any more rude or aggressive than plenty of other uses of speech like slow sarcasm or patronising explanation but today the mantra didn't release any of the constriction that was choking him as surely as a strangler squeezing his adam's apple with a meaty fist.

When he got back to his flat, noticing as if for the first time the drab emptiness of it, the long-suppressed isolation that echoed, reverberating around the walls, his eyes searched for signs of comfort. There was literally nothing that caught his attention as worthy of preserving. And yet he feared the absence of it, the home he had created for himself, this empty space. He needed some sound advice. He didn't know who he could call on, none of his friends were on that level for him and he'd blown it with Belle, but she wasn't the right person anyway.

Thursday evening, why was that ringing a bell? Kung Fu class and Gus. With that thought Matt picked up phone and keys and heard the door slam behind him taking the stairs a couple at a time.

He entered the hall just as Gus was finishing up the introductions. There were about twelve other students in the class. They stared inquisitively at the late comer and Gus, sensitive to energetic balance subtly caught their attention giving Matt time to find a space and start to focus. A couple of familiar faces nodded. The warmup exercise was breath work. Matt started to calm feeling for the easy familiarity he had experienced the first time in class, the warming sense of molten honey. It was hard won. The tension was ossified showing him the extent of his rigidity. With each move as if quietly blowing on the fragile spark of a fire he gradually started to feel more flexible and fluid. Why he hadn't got around to practising this was now impossible to remember. Every so often Gus smiled encouragement at him and by the time they finished the first sets, much of the day's stress had dissipated.

'We all carry a lot of tension in our bodies' Gus was saying as if reading his mind, 'some of it is necessary of course otherwise we couldn't function, but the trick is to recognise the tension in the mind and relax that cos otherwise it'll rule you and while you're busy stressing out the other bugger'll have you!'

The class laughed and Gus invited one of them to act as his accomplice to demonstrate moves that they would then practice.

'OK partner up,' he called after showing the specifics of the attack and defence postures.

The guy who had been standing next to Matt moved away to work with someone else, and as the other members of the group doubled up in pairs Matt saw a young woman walk a little nervously towards him. She had shoulder length black hair, a neat body, and a slightly shy downward gaze.

'Shall we?' she said tucking a strand of hair behind her ear in what looked like a habitual movement. Her eyes were green when she lifted her gaze to speak and her voice gave something of her away: she sounded educated, and the sportswear spoke of a comfortable wage.

'Remember,' said Gus as the chatter of the class died down following the bustle of finding someone to work with, 'our bodies speak a language, our gestures and stance tell our opponents a lot about us. Become aware of what you're putting out and read your partner's movements, they are broadcasting their intentions. We all are, we can't help it, but once you wake up to the fact you can use your subtle awareness to your advantage.'

Matt took up a stance and the woman approached to deliver a punch, he raised his forearm and deflected the attack. It was all very controlled, and they were instructed to repeat. After a few attempts they both started to relax and elaborate the initially wooden movements into something more lifelike and animated, relevant to potential real-life encounters. They smiled, satisfied with the successful execution of the postures.

'Swop around now,' Gus instructed.

As the woman stood now ready in defence Matt noticed a significant difference in her as if she was habitually in this posture of self-protection. He delivered his punch carefully so as not to aggravate the sense of her having disappeared into a shell. She deflected a little too quickly reaching out and losing her grounded centre of gravity.

'Wait for it,' Matt found himself teasing her grinning.

She scowled almost imperceptibly, it was subtle but obvious she hadn't appreciated the familiarity, the shell grew thicker, the rapport of a few moments before evaporated. They finished the rest of the exercise in silence with little enthusiasm. Jarred by the feeling he had offended her whilst smarting with a sense that she felt herself superior he brushed it off as she walked back to the opposite corner of the hall. Volumes of information were filling the space yet barely a sentence had passed between them. The class finished shortly after and once again the invite for a drink was extended and once again Matt chose to decline. He couldn't talk to Gus about his predicament while a gang of other students were around him, and since his earlier panic had now subsided to a dull background anxiety, he'd thought twice about it realising it might not be wise to let him know what kind of business he was involved in. For all he knew Gus might be an off-duty policeman.

Matt was strategizing all the way home. The end of the week had they said, when exactly was that? Tomorrow was Friday but they could wait until the end of the weekend or at least until he'd got it clear in his head. He had never had much cause to think too deeply about the business he couriered for. It was just a means to an end. Being a lowly mouse to the boss's eagle it hadn't yet crossed his mind to feel undue concern. The issue for him wasn't being on wrong side of the law, that was hypocrisy in his opinion, after all the business wasn't any different from any other supply and demand chain, but he had heard plenty of whispers from other guys. You were stupid if too innocent of the rumours of harsh beatings and callous reprisals if you stepped out of line, but he had always figured or maybe secretly hoped these were exaggerated tales cobbled together from too many cartel movies and hard man talk. He couldn't quite dispel the belief however that the men in the pub that day had seen and caused their fair share of vicious violence when their bidding wasn't done. Deep down he had known this moment was coming. He'd been biding his time until something happened that would force him to stare it in the face. His life had become a hollow approximation of what he would truly like it to be, he wasn't satisfied with a natural progression of the negligence of his younger experience. He had deliberately steered clear of any gang involvement preferring instead to simply trust to himself, this had been the way he'd coped, ploughing a furrow head down avoiding confrontation through efficiency. He hadn't seen the wall until he hit it. About to reach for his stash to roll a joint he stopped himself. Instinctively refraining from this habit gave him an unexpected surge of clarity. He slowed his breathing as they had done at the beginning of class and found a curious lightness pervade him. As if pulsing through the curtains it even imbued the bedraggled cushions and the lack lustre sofa with a stream of luminescence that now seemed to filter through his body and charge his cells with calm and an incredibly spacious sense of expansion. The edges of his being seemed to be merging into the space around it. He gazed uncomprehendingly at his hands and in that moment the spell was broken. Shocked back into the mundane he was immediately regretful, so he focused his breath once again and although less forceful felt the calming union once again descend. The love of a mother, he found himself saying out aloud, the love of the mother. It had been so long, so lonely and yet now in this extraordinary moment he couldn't remember why, feeling as he did a glorious visitation of graceful peace.

☐

The nights were drawing in with gathering speed, falling towards the darkness of winter as leaves cast off their moorings to rot under trees and the spindles of branches punctured the sky.

He parked in the little carpark and headed off across the common. Only now did it occur to him that perhaps he might not be welcome at this time in the late afternoon, but the day had flown by, and the Friday traffic had delayed his exit from the city even further. She could always say it wasn't convenient. There was a single light at the upper window of the cottage otherwise everything was twilit. Matt could hear a quiet voice coming through the single pane, a gentle song lonely and unguarded. He coughed theatrically in warning to announce himself, embarrassed now to intrude on the melancholy of the moment. Wanting to run but seeing a light turn on in the hall he called out.

'Karen? It's Matt, I met you the other day, sorry to just turn up like this I was in the area and thought I'd say hello.'

He heard a muffled response and moments later the door opened. Karen stood with the light behind her awkwardly composing herself, hands smoothing down her jumper then reaching up to adjust her hair.

'I'm sorry to just turn up…' Matt repeated, his voice trailing off as he tried to work out what was different about her.

'Oh it's you,' she said disturbed from solitude and only just now recognising him, 'no problem, come right on in.' She stepped aside and swept an arm gesturing welcome, a slight slur to her voice as if the velvet was ruffled.

'I've been flirting with the underworld, she said, this time of year sometimes gets to me. Want to join me?'

She held up a half empty bottle of red wine.

'I know it's a bit early,' she teased him with an exaggerated wink 'but as soon as it's getting dark, I reckon that's the right time to take the edge off the blues with a red.'

'I won't thanks, I'm driving. And to be honest, I'm not much of a drinker.'

'Ah! You prefer the other stuff, can't fool me. Let me put the kettle on then. I'll join you for a cuppa, probably better anyway else I'll get completely pissed and I'd much rather talk to you.'

She appeared to snap out of the mild intoxication with the ease of a cat leaping from sofa to windowsill, one moment lounging in liquid, the next alert and ready to pounce. Soon they and the awkward initial moments were settled by the flickering flames of the wood burner hands cupped around mugs. Karen passed him the biscuit tin and bit into one herself, crumbs cascading down her jumper. She swiped them languidly onto the hearthside rug, 'treats for the mice, which in turn will be treats for the cats. So, my new friend, what brings you here? You said you were in the area, up to your mysterious encounters?'

Either the wine had loosened her tongue or else this sharp perception was who she was. Matt decided to put down any pretence.

'Actually, that was a lie. I came specially to see you. Those mysterious encounters, I need someone to talk to about them.' He laughed nervously. 'I'm in trouble. I need advice.'

'Well, I'm honoured that you thought of me. As must be completely obvious by now, I too could do with the company, alone and drinking in the afternoon….and it's been a long time since anyone asked my help about anything,' her voice became quiet and serious, 'but I will do my best to be straightforward and true if you tell me what's bothering you.'

Slowly Matt started to explain his predicament. Without too much incriminating detail he explained how inadvertently he had found himself in a trap, unsure how to escape, what would happen to him if he turned down the promotion. Feeling strangely safe in the confidence of this unknown woman, he continued unburdening the troubles of a lifetime, it required no forethought. Telling his story in this way clarified the narrative he had made of it. Almost as soon as he had told one chapter, he was aware that he could have emphasised it slightly differently to achieve a different result. The manipulation of detail, the shade, exposure, focus creates an infinitely variable story, choice of perspective is everything. Matt didn't want to either portray himself or be perceived as victim. Long years of self-reliance had held him steady; he wasn't going to give that up for anyone even as the release of endurance into language created new vulnerability. Karen sat cradling her long drained mug and staring into the flames of the wood burner, occasionally nodding, or murmuring encouragement and sympathy. At one moment tears swelled in her eyes and he found himself wanting to comfort her, apologising.

'Not at all sweetheart, tears are good. I need them just as much as you do. Please don't deny me, go on.'

It was properly dark outside when he'd finished laying out the details of his life as an archaeologist might with the scattered bones of an unexpected skeleton. A single point of light was anchored in his centre and multiple tangential threads were beaming off at every angle, the accumulation of his experience pieced together Matt sat completely still as if shocked by it. The cul de sac of the current predicament fitted perfectly into the street map he'd been walking through. He sat back on the raggedy old sofa with its woollen throws hiding worn through cat scratches, firelight flickering gently. It pulsed to the sounds and cadence of the flames' combustion as they gobbled up the story.

'Well, that is quite some tale.' Karen ventured after a long pause. She blew her nose.

'I'd like to congratulate you on your survival skills.' Her voice wavered, 'what a lot you had to deal with. You would never guess to look at you.'

'What's that supposed to mean?' Matt reacted; the room's peace shattered.

'Easy love, I'm sorry, I meant that it would be impossible to know how much you've been through, you don't give any of it away on the outside.' Karen coaxed him as she might a cat who had unexpectedly released its claws. 'You're bound to feel tender and a bit sore now having shared all that with me, I'm just a bit of a sad outcast not a therapist. She apologised again. But I promise you this, there is nothing in what you have told me that I don't sympathise with and if we put our heads together, we'll work out a strategy, I like a challenge and I can't stand a bully. A problem shared is a problem halved.' An awkward smile flexed her mouth, but her eyes remained sad.

Matt shrugged; the hurt of the little boy was telescoped in time collapsing the confidence of earlier. They sat again in silence waiting for the ripples to dissipate after the pebble had fractured a fragile surface.

'Do you fancy some cheese on toast?' Said Karen suddenly, 'I'm starving.'

'Yes please.' Matt smiled. 'I haven't eaten since breakfast apart from that biscuit and for the record,' he added, 'you're much better at listening than any of the so-called professionals I've had to see.'

Chapter ten

Sean hadn't got up for a week. Pockmarked punctured plastic lay crumpled by the side of the unmade bed in the spare room that he'd moved into, the diazepam packet was now empty. The loss of his efficient work routine had spiralled his identity effortlessly down the plughole. Without it to prop him up he was adrift, gurgling through a sewage system, unwanted waste. Cathy and the kids gave him a wide berth as he lay growling, a retired circus tiger in his den.

In many ways it was easier for them to have him thus incapacitated, they could move freely through their days without having to navigate his orders. The tension of their various relationships had however merely transformed. A passively aggressive cloud emanated from beneath the doorway of the small front bedroom as if through the bars of a cage. It appeared to extend mistily along the landing before dispersing around the bathroom. Sometimes hot as steam, at others a freezing patch issued a warning: give a wide berth to whoever their dad was becoming as he lay behind that door.

He wasn't in pain as such, he simply didn't know what to do to move the spillage of his body. Subsequently, simple daily tasks like taking a shower or popping a couple of slices of bread into the toaster had become gargantuan. He spent long moments staring at the back of his hands then in a moment of apparent inspiration might turn them over and gaze into the palms as if the meaning of his condition could be found there. He had become a carcass, unplugged, socket less, and without any energy. The medication had been consumed without obvious effect and he had lost track of the follow up doctor's appointment through lack of will and belief in any forthcoming help although he would have been hard pressed to remember even if he had wanted to attend. To say he was depressed wasn't accurate. Low mood didn't cover it either as he wasn't able to reflect upon himself. It was as if he'd gone out and forgotten how to come home. Some people might say he was suffering from a loss of his soul.

His wife took her concerns to the weekly counselling session where she explored the ongoing effect he had on her life. She had been going to counselling for years on and off in an attempt to deal with loveless family life in general and her marriage in particular. She had seen patterns connecting her choice of husband with the men in her family of origin. Her husband's recent deterioration only changed her understanding in so far as he had become like a different flavour of crisps, formerly salt and vinegar and now prawn cocktail: bad for her health but easy to snack on when you couldn't be bothered to cook. The kids appeared to carry on regardless, off to school after squabbling at the breakfast table, incessantly scrolling through tiktok and snapchat when they weren't watching TV or facetiming friends. It was seamless how effectively he had disappeared from the day to day of their lives and equally horrifying, because in some shadowy corner that the light from their screens didn't allow them to see, the lack of his presence lurked. Imprisoned and dislocated.

◻

Flexing sinew, muscle, and bone to the rhythm synchronising from inside the music and out, the sheer joy of pulsing blood, to abandon all caution and self-consciousness, Belle was going out dancing. Of all her favourite activities dancing was top of the list. It was far less complicated than sex and way more easily liberating. Life was simply to be lived and what better way to live than to dance, this she concluded after the annoying waste of energy she had expended thinking about Matt and his motives.

Finishing off her flared turquoise jumpsuit with a pair of sparkling false eyelashes she laughed at her reflection, pouting stupid selfie style before donning her sensible coat against the cold winter night and clunking out the front door on stack heels.

The thing about intimate relationships she reasoned is that so much is loaded on to them, the expectations of desire and durability seemed to clash. Casual sex was supposedly easy, and it was sort of expected that you'd end up in bed with whoever took your fancy after a night out, order from a menu, browse a buffet bar, pick what you liked. But she simply couldn't pretend that it worked like that for her. She wanted to be more careful. Find someone who could properly care for her, get to know them before the hormones chose for you. All but her closest friends accused her of insecurity and frumpiness but when it came to relaxing about her body in naked proximity to another's she knew herself well enough that the depressing drunken comedown was not worth revisiting. She had learned to regret intimacy while under the influence. It smacked of desperation. She had misjudged and trusted unreliable characters far too often. Take Matt for example, she had felt so sure they had recognised a mutual unspoken similarity that his failure to follow through had been thoroughly disappointing and caused her to question and re-evaluate her judgment yet again. She was heartily sick of all that. She was dressed up and would dance instead.

Caught in a wind tunnel the reinforced plastic bus shelter timetables were smeary with scratches and rendered illegible. She shivered: underneath the quilted coat the thin fabric of her flimsy going out clothes lacked insulation. Stamping the heavy shoes, unsure how long she would need to keep circulation going against the biting wind she forced her mind away from turbulent thoughts towards the night ahead. The yellow tunnels of bus headlights were turning a corner further down the road piercing the night with their approach. As the bus drew near, Belle recognised one of the shop's regulars sitting behind the wheel.

'Looking good tonight Belle!' Smiling at the driver, she walked down the half empty bus and leaving behind the moment of melancholy, relaxed into the warmth.

☐

At home in her flat Alice, bone weary, was writing up yet another unwanted child's case study report. Another fragile little one was bearing the brunt of failure to nurture and love. Clouded links of genetic chains were clanging from one generation into the next endlessly hobbling hope, dragging balls of pain along with them. Her elbows on the desk, spot lit by a glowing pool from the lamp she combed back dark hair in a gesture of dejected surrender. Her hands reached the top of her head, and her face sank down. All that was holding her up was a mechanical balance from elbow to skull. As students in training, they had studied sociology and psychology to be able to act compassionately in challenging circumstances. The ologies did not however prepare you for the onslaught of feelings in reaction to an encounter with a skeletally thin grey skinned five-year-old in sodden nappies, who nobody was feeding, knowing that the violent boyfriend of the out of it mum was sitting them on his knee while he wanked off to a porn channel. The blank, scabby awfulness of it slurped at any dregs of sympathy left in Alice's empty glass. Sometimes there was no wider perspective to reach into to stabilise and rebalance. She wanted to give this up, acknowledge that she didn't have what it took to work in the harshness of that grim world and still care. All the education, expectations and aspiration to become a professional somebody was as insubstantial as dandelion fluff on the breeze, she couldn't see straight enough to reach out and catch them airborne, to make a wish, to escape. Exhausted she rested her forehead on a forearm as the jargon of outcomes and risks, responsibilities and budgets floated like scum rising to the boil in a pan of dirty water.

Plummeting suddenly downwards she found herself in a catacomb that was hidden underground. Dusty skulls and jutting femurs protruded from decaying columns of sandy stone. Shrieks and yells spun off like electricity along darkened tunnels of despair as an impending sense of catastrophe and panic filled the network of interlacing pathways. Fuelled by a sickening sense of inadequacy she watched helpless as the smell of squalor, of lack of hygiene, unwashed bodies and sodden mattresses, faeces and vomit, piles of washing up and rodent droppings invaded the decaying alleys. Rot and disintegration multiplied at incredible speed until the tunnels were drowning. Waves of churning feelings tumbled all images of decency, degradation, purity, and poverty into a vast sea of possibilities. There was no way up, nor down. Ghosts drifted derelict as fragmented imagery of enslavement, hangings, deportation, wars, burnings, starvation, torture, and mutilation connected them with once living human shapes. Dark entities, unrecognisable in form, lurked suggestively around the peripheries whispering deep memories of coercion to the silent fleeting figures mocking them in their entrapment. Ancestors, where are you, called another voice, it's time to show us, come and bear witness. And they appeared one after the other, couple by couple like animals into the ark, in an ever-increasing expanding pattern. Lords and ladies, peasants and paupers, racketeers and philanthropists, learners, know it alls, advisors, instructors, those that do their bidding, losers, the helpless, the harsh and the cruel, the shining winners, the great hearted, the transcendent, the wilted, the lost, the found, the meek, the forthright.

All of humanity's diverse expressions clustered aound bearing their children, bearing their births and deaths, opening, and closing pulsing hearts to the joys and the miseries of years branching exponentially into the great world tree of everyone and everything, everywhere connected by spiralling filaments of genetic strands into a vast and complete web, the myriad forms recycling through mysteries. Flowers began to blossom in the corridors. Massive bouquets of wild and generous flowers, lustrous peonies, budding roses, fanfaring daffodils, gorgeous violets, soft petalled pinks, delicate fresias, daisies, magnolias, jasmine, and jonquil. Flowerheads and stems of all imaginable colours, fragrant and welcoming seemed to inhabit every available space in what now appeared to be a florists' shop. People were holding great bunches of exquisite arrangements to share their love and care with the artistry of an invisible florist. Their arms were full, the abundance overwhelming as the bunches then shapeshifted into light and the light into forms that were comforting all cries of suffering, of incarnation and time.

Alice's neck was cricked awkwardly against a tilted elbow, her face scrunched against the desk's hard surface. Rubbing circulation back into her neck and face she gently sobbed the dream images from her. They left through tears coursing down her sad cheeks, in rivulets of stress that scoured the surface of her skin. Once deposited back into the pool of lamp light in her living room, desk, chair, sofa, all standing solidly by, she needed to get to bed. She had been hoping for a good night's sleep, tomorrow early, despite it being the weekend she had an emergency video case conference. Non-attendance wasn't an option.

☐

Matt was now walking back across the common. The sky was freshly poured into a darkening glass and ancient stars perforated the firmament like bubbles defying time. Thousands of years of scattered light now pin pricked his skin. Was light in its entirety obscured by an enormous dark blanket whose weave let faraway beams penetrate through the intersections in the fabric? A fingernail of moon made a bracket towards the west.

They hadn't exactly made a plan, but Karen had offered her best strategy.

"Basically, they are a bunch of bullies' she had concluded simply 'and on no account do you give in to the fear that they are trying to manipulate you with.'

'Well, that's easy for you to say he had countered but I know what these guys are capable of, and I don't want to end up carved up and thrown to their attack dogs.'

'Of course you don't,' she had said, mindful of his earlier defensiveness. 'So, disappear for a bit, lie low for a while, throw away that horrible work phone. Tell them you appreciate the offer, but you've been made a better one. Give it some time and you'll soon be history and not in the way you're thinking.'

'I can't do that.'

'Why not?'

'I need a car, a job, a place to live, food, what about my flat?'

'Move out, give it up. Go away somewhere they can't trace you, you said yourself that you weren't happy with it all.'

He had shaken his head. 'It's not that easy,' then more quietly, 'I don't know where I would go.'

Before Karen knew what she was going to say the words spoke for themselves: 'You could come and stay here.' She wondered who it was talking until she caught up with the one who had done the inviting and added practically, 'I could do with some help around the place, in the garden, chopping logs, fixing a few bits and pieces. We can agree an exchange. There's plenty of space. Just for a while until the heat is over for you. I'm not suggesting anything permanent.'

Here she had waited until impatience nudged her further: 'How about it, we help each other out, isn't this the way to make the world work? If we don't make the leap, we'll never fly.'

Matt said he'd have to think about it. He didn't have a passport and he didn't have another place to go. In truth he was hardly able to hear Karen's offer, the idea that a stranger would want to help him wasn't easily translated, it might as well have been spoken in a foreign language. Taking down her phone number he had thanked her and then suddenly wanting to get out before being overwhelmed by the warming fire and a free fall feeling of rudderless chaos, he had got up to leave.

Walking in the cool night air across the land he slowed his pace. Felt the cold night bathe his skin, the sharpness of the stars. The lack of speed settled him. He rarely felt unhurried in the city, some level of guard was always necessary. He needed to take his time.

But as Matt drove back to the city he was again muddied by doubt. The roads were clear and as he played with the idea of saying yes to the boss men he imagined himself mercury in a thermometer rising towards fever, moving up the ranks accumulating greater levels of power, money, recognition, his body tensed, jaw tightening in the familiarity of adrenaline, he could do it. By the time he arrived back at the flat just past midnight, however, the fantasy fortune had so tarnished with stress imagined weapons, airports, danger, and reprisals he had changed his mind. The price was crazily high whichever direction he looked. But in the balance, he had to bid for freedom. Checking his finances, he was relieved to find that he had almost five grand in the bank. He would need to get out some cash but after tonight he couldn't be using traceable ATMs. Perhaps transfer a lump over to Karen, leaving enough to keep the account open even if it then lay dormant. He knew that the organisation employed hackers who could break into any system. He texted for her bank details and to say he'd be arriving later. Next, after brewing coffee to sustain the effort, he sent an email to the letting agency giving notice on the lease of his flat, they could have the deposit in lieu of any rent.

The letting agents kept a spare set of keys so he could lock up and leave. That would ensure he didn't bottle out. An incongruous feeling was starting to bubble up inside him as if a jacuzzi had been turned on and the fizzing froth was tickling his insides. He kept doubts back with a steady force of will, policing the barricade at any unruly resistance. He rested rather than slept and around dawn was packing up the car with the few possessions that were of value to him: clothes, music speaker, computer, a couple of old framed photos, some bedding, toiletries. It all fitted into a couple of black bin bags. Karen's place was small and besides he had the momentum now, didn't want any excess baggage. From each abandoned domestic object that he had bought to construct a home he now felt an unhooking: the potato masher, lamp, bathmat, mirror: they were all that had tethered him, he could simply leave them behind. He cleaned up the ashtray and on a strange whim decided to dust and wipe as many surfaces as thoroughly as he could. He wouldn't put it past the boss man to tip off the police about illegal activity at this address even though it was his car where all the business was ever conducted and there wasn't anything in the flat that a forensic team could identify other than a bit of personal use blow. Thinking about the car, pressure increased. The car was his getaway, but it was traceable. He'd have to sort that later. He tapped the brief message into his work mobile and pressed send just as creeping morning light filtered into the winter day. *Ray, I'm not in.* He had let them know by the weekend after all. Wiping all texts and contacts he removed the sim card from the phone and bagged it with the rest of the rubbish, taking it out with him as he locked the door then, mentally checking everything he needed was the right side of the door, he lifted the flap of the letterbox and posted the keys. He heard their tinkling thud hit the mat as he left.

☐

Karen battled thoughts as sleep evaded her: what was she thinking inviting a near stranger to share her privacy and space, it was dangerously trusting. However much she had warmed to Matt he was nevertheless an unknown quantity, and though his life story had moved her to compassion, recklessly opening her door to a dealer on the run from a drug baron, without any sense of her own boundaries smacked of desperation. What kind of trouble would he bring with him? Her cottage was small, even an excellent actor couldn't keep up a façade in such a small space. He might turn out to be a nasty piece of work needing an out of the way place to conduct a heist and she'd fallen right into his trap. She saw herself held hostage by her own stupid ignorance. But this was exactly the kind of smallminded fantasy thinking she abhorred. What was life if limited to a fearful little self, filling time, passing judgment, scared of possibility. When exactly had her horizons narrowed to become an ivy cataracted window with only half-light visible? No, she wouldn't shrink from a new challenge, she would prefer to be dead or murdered by misplaced trust than this insipid approximation of life. However it turned out would be more interesting than ongoing monotony pretending contentment. Her slender fingers reached from under the quilt to click off the sleepless lamp as the morning light seeped into the room. Adventure would be arriving. She would welcome it.

Chapter eleven

Belle and her friends had all agreed on the jump suits. There were rainbow coloured options in the end of line stock sale. The onesy had had its day. Lots of big babies in velour romper suits had worn out its attraction, but the jump suit had a touch more class, a nod to 70's retro that hoped to redeem itself from pyjamaland to superpower. Somewhere many miles away other women had sat at sewing machines, their dextrous fingers nimbly running up the remaindered cloth into garments sold for bargain basement prices, their wages probably equivalent to a round of drinks at the night out for which the costumes were created. The young women who met outside the club were friends from school, they had looked out for each other through all the heart aches and losses of adolescence. Now as they were growing older some cracks were beginning to form in the mortar of their unquestioned loyalties. Opinions were taking shape, creating subsidence where former foundations had lain rock solid. Uncomfortable differences whispered about later between factions divided by invisible conditions. But shrieking now in delight at the multi coloured collection cladding their different body shapes with uniform lycra, they were together and glad to be so. Belle's best friend was Lisa dressed tonight in fuchsia pink, they hugged, excited to show each other details of their outfits. The queue at the door was often remembered later as the best bit of the night, when comparing clothes and make up, hopping on high heels to ward of the chill of the night, there was still the exciting prospect of an unknown evening ahead. Once the dark doors had swallowed them and the vibe of the night revealed itself, the thrill of anticipation was over. Whether the night yielded pure fun or overindulgence and disappointment was a roulette table of haphazard forces including chemical enhancement, mood, encounters, and positions of the planets. Inevitably yet another post mortem would be required when the effects wore off the following morning. It was the ritual of it all that was the spell binder and usually the deciding factor for Belle was the quality of the DJ. The festoon lights above the doorway created a dressing room mirror glamour and two bouncers stood handsomely sentinel at the entrance, with black coats and earbuds their costume and accessories. The queue stretched along the building waiting to meet them and be admitted like guests at a wedding. When Belle's group reached the door, one of them raised his hand responding to an inaudible message. He was a big guy, clean shaven from chin to nape of neck as if put through a carwash of razors, polished then dowsed in aftershave.

'Just a moment Ladies, won't keep you long' he explained winking. 'Nice outfits' he added with a slight lick of his lips. The other bouncer grinned catching Belle's eye. He rolled his eyes in mockery of his colleague's leer, exasperated by the predictability of it. Belle smiled back pulling a momentarily twisted grimace and an unexpected tender sympathy passed between them. He seemed poised, comfortable in his skin, like a big cat, standing easily but gracefully ready, hair curling on his coat collar, eyes alert, a quiet smile beaming through them.

The first bouncer, self-importantly responding to an inner ear instruction waved them on and as Belle stepped up through the doorway following her friends, the other simply said 'Enjoy yourself.' His voice was steadily assured and innocently seductive as she felt him genuinely wishing her pleasure. A jolt of electricity followed the jumpsuit's torso and Belle slowed down to integrate it. Lisa turned back to check her as she fell out of step. 'You alright Belle?' 'Sure. Never better.' Belle smiled with a readjusting cough, slightly surprised that she didn't want to share that little moment with her bestie. Later when they poured along the street in a stream of relaxed pleasure, even the grime of the wheely bins overspilling takeaway detritus onto the pavement couldn't dim their glow.

'That was the best night I can remember in a long while.' Lisa linked arms with Belle and tucked her head into her friend's shoulder. 'You were on fire girl, what a mover!'

'Not so bad yourself....'

'I totally LOVED that DJ who was she?'

'Not a clue, but me too, everyone a winner baby!'

And they laughed, sang and frolicked on tired shoes all the way to the bus stop as the night's dark dissolved shade by shade to the pallor of pale winter skin. Inside Belle was the memory of the bouncer's quiet warm presence. He had passed her on the dance floor on his way to quiet down a ruckus. With the merest shiver of a move, he had fluidly joined her shifting form. It was a playful tease, no sense of threat and one that she had wished to prolong, to carry on playing the dance game with each other.

☐

The morning case conference was tediously bureaucratic. The system was a gluttonous monster hungrily devouring details of endless referrals and inter agency communications in an impenetrable cave of protocols. Alice was impatient for it to be over. Despite having slept deeply and uneventfully for a full nine hours she had woken with the shadowy shroud of her dream weighing her down into the mattress. She waited until the last moment to sit up and turn on the computer. She had pulled on a jumper and quickly brushed her hair. It was one of the dubious perks of the zoom era that you could be semi naked or still in your pyjamas as long as the portion of screen showed a wide-awake professional. Sometimes she thought it had made her worse at her job, reduced to a virtual rectangle that cut out the need to present herself whole to the world. Pretence was now an accepted part of working practice, they all did it, toes stroking the dog under the table, a crossword puzzle on the lap when it wasn't your turn to talk. Perhaps the pretence had been there all along, merely hidden behind different choices of tailoring, different working scenery. She longed to be somewhere green and natural, somewhere no humans could make demands on her. Perhaps the cool shelter of a cathedral of trees where light dapples the congregation under the blessings of branches. Or a wide-open hillside heath overviewing lowland where her head could clear unfettered into the sky and she, wide open could consider her options. Although it was a bit of a drive away, she knew of a quiet hill that was both majestic, but little visited. There an iron age hill fort giving a vantage point that overlooked a broad and wooded valley with another range of hills on the distant horizon. It beckoned to her in her mind's eye. She smiled, gently relieved to know where she was going, remembering 'give me some space!' had been her shouted teenage mantra whenever she felt overwhelmed. Her parents were well meaning but as an only child she had experienced the full force of their neurotic parenting skills as they juggled childminders and afterschool provision once her granny was dead. At weekends they would over involve themselves with her when they weren't at work just as she was trying to relax after the rigorous round of after school activities during the week. She knew this was so-called privilege, all the classes: swimming, riding, music, rock climbing, she'd tried them all, not out of interest but to keep her occupied and looked after, there was never a moment's downtime in a gruelling schedule. As soon as the zoom call was over, she showered and dressed in walking gear and trainers, taking walking boots in a separate bag, along with a flask of hot tea and sandwich for later. She liked having clothes for different activities, they were costumes that delineated free time, protecting her from thoughts of others' needs, she could become that walker or kung fu practitioner or salsa dancer with the help of the disguise.

Granny Myra had been the first to put the idea into her impressionable mind, teaching how people treat you differently depending on what you wear.

'Especially,' she had laughed, 'as you get older, when they don't much look beyond your grey hair and wrinkles.' They had even done some experiments going on little outings together, carefully choosing clothes to create a desired impression, it was all about the impression granny had said, because people assume all sorts of things even before they have actively thought them. One day Myra had deliberately not brushed her or Alice's hair when they went to the shops, leaving signs of breakfast around their mouths and chins, they had queued for ages before anyone served them. Another time they had chosen their smarts as she had called them, applying subtle make up, perfume and extra jewellery just to take the cat to the vets.

'Good morning, ladies' the vet had said mock bowing.

They had laughed afterwards giggling conspiratorially. Thinking about it now Alice realised it was advanced psychology in action and just how astute her granny had been. She would have had something to say about zoom meetings. The morning soothed her with a winter grey that boded well for walking weather. She headed out of town on the northbound motorway, the speed of the car pressing through rushing air comforted her as all the other vehicles whizzed past anonymously demanding nothing from her save that she kept out of their way.

Matt arrived back at the common by Karen's cottage punch-drunk and reeling from all the coming and going, the fizzy adrenaline evaporated. He parked in the little car park, turned off the engine and utterly blank, slumped in a post rush. As if the decisions had been made from somewhere remote and he, radio controlled, had woken up in an alternate reality with batteries drained. Resting his head on the steering wheel he took in a slow breath and exhaled feeling the desire to scream gently recede as the breathing compelled him into each moment by moment. It was ok, it would be ok, everything was ok, it would be alright. But the flat gone, a stranger's home, the car, the numberplate it was a public place, what if he was followed……. it's ok, it would be ok, everything will work out ok it's going to be alright. The breathing Gus had taught slowly began to calm him, steadying his nerves, the lack of sleep and the seesaw journeying, taming the wild horse startled by a gun crack.

A pale green car drew up beside his and the driver turned off the engine. He was immediately alert. Oh god this had been a bad idea, the pull to panic was a rip tide but losing it had never saved anyone from drowning, so he resisted, forcing himself to breathe the sense of out-of-control spiral down again, he rode the wave, a hurricane twisting itself to earth, and glanced over at the driver getting out of the vehicle. If he had been shocked a moment before nothing could have prepared him for the stun of recognition that punched through him as the dark-haired woman from the kung fu class opened the boot and sat to put on her walking boots. Perhaps it was the comfort of some semblance of familiarity or the surreal shock of incongruous coincidence, but he opened his car door and stepped out moving cautiously towards her.

'Kung fu right? Gus's class.'

If he was shocked, she looked horrified to be met and spoken to in this unlikely location. She sat speechless.

'Sorry,' he stammered. 'I didn't mean to intrude I was just so surprised to see someone I recognised here of all places.'

'Me too,' she managed and just about smiled. If there was an archetypal visual for a lost child, that smile would be it. The set of her mouth spoke of disappointed resolve, of a tragic twist in the plot. In the one facial movement he recognised a historical loneliness.

'I'm Matt' he said intuitively wanting to relieve them of the all-pervading awkwardness, 'we didn't even introduce ourselves in the class.'

'My name's Alice.' She responded holding out her hand in polite greeting. 'What are you doing here?'

'That's tricky to explain,' he stammered again, not having expected to have to explain anything to anybody, 'I'm not being funny, just it's a bit complicated and…..' he tailed off.

'My turn to apologise, I don't need to know. I'm just out for a walk, this is a place I come to when I need some space. Workload destress.' She shrugged then finished lacing her boots and slung a rucksack over her shoulder. 'I'll set off then. I hope whatever it is proves manageable for you. See you at class sometime?'

'Er, I probably won't be back there anytime soon.' Shit, now he sounded evasive, suspicious even…

'Oh right, well see you whenever then.' And she strode off through the gate onto the common leaving him feeling as if a precious opportunity had just jumped off a cliff. She walked away wondering about the obvious stress pulsing out from him like a high-pressure jet spray, the same person who had seemed so confident and cocky when they'd met in that lesson. Her professional nose sniffed something less than straightforward. Matt sat back in the car in shock. Bumping into a familiar face in what he had fled to as a secure hideout was a side swipe. It was the second time Alice had thrown him off kilter, but although the coincidence was disconcerting it had at least tripped up the panic and shoved it off stage. As he emptied the boot, he pondered the sad smile and wondered if he had misjudged Alice's aloofness. He started walking across towards the cottage, swinging the two bin liners one from each hand, creating a pendulum effect as they left right in turn propelled him forwards. Reaching the rickety wooden gate, he clicked open the latch and pushed, watching as it dropped off rotten at the lower hinge. The garden was seasonally quiet, settling down for a good long sleep, seeds tucked in, gestating deep in the dark of cold earth, rotting leaves its surface blanket. He glanced over at the horizon and drew in a cool draught of the chilly air. Only just now did it fully dawn on him what a generous offer he had been gifted and tapping the door resolved to show Karen all the gratitude he could muster.

The spare room had a sloping roof where the eaves of the cottage met the little dormer window. It was big enough for the small double with the iron bedstead that Karen had picked up at an auction when she first moved in. She thought it would suit the oldy woldy cottagey style and that she might even get round to making a patchwork quilt from scraps of cloth cut from her cast off clothes to complete the scene. This had never happened, and she now wondered if anyone had ever actually slept in it. Beside the bed was a lamp on a rickety stool, the wire bound up with electrical tape like a cartoon finger bandage. The room smelt damp and the mattress was cold with unevaporated moisture. There was a small alcove for hanging clothes but no space for any other furniture, he'd have to keep his bag under the bed. She sighed, seeing the fantasy idyll for what it was. It was at least a space and Matt could make of it what he would. She left the door ajar hoping that any feeble heat from the rest of the house might waft its way upstairs.

They would have to have some house rules, there were certain things that it would be better to have clear before they started.

The toilet seat, please don't leave it up. The kitchen, wash up after yourself, leave it as you found it. She had cleared her experiments with mouldering leftovers and wiped down the surfaces, but she wasn't going to tidy up anyone else's mess. No smoking in the house and definitely no drugs. She looked at the recycling bag bulging with wine bottles, she'd take this as a cue to cut down. No random guests unless she had met them already. Be nice to the cats, it was their home first.

She realised she was fidgeting and glanced at the clock on the cooker. He'd said to expect him back by late morning. Just enough time to compose herself and make it look like she really was as cool as she hoped he thought she was. He knocked the door, bin bags in hands.

Chapter twelve

Sean's phone had been silent for the last fortnight. Nobody was wanting to ring him. At work they were glad of his absence and his drinking mates had disappeared as quickly as a first pint. When the once familiar New York taxi horn ringtone startled him awake this morning he wasn't entirely sure he wasn't still dreaming. He grasped eagerly after the sound, frisking the bedside table with a clumsy hand motivated by a drowning desperation for contact.

'Hello,' his tongue was furred, his throat sticky dry.

'Sean, me ol fella, how's tricks?'

'Who's this now?' Sean was trying to focus to put a face to the voice.

'What, you don't recognise your own brother-in-law? Cathy said you were rough, but I didn't realise you'd gone gaga, it's Ray.'

'Oh Ray, hi, what do you want?'

'Now now, Sean, be nice, it's customary to have a few pleasantries before we get down to business.'

'What kind of business Ray, I'm off sick.'

'Yes, so I heard. I was thinking of dropping by. You busy?'

Sean wanted to tell him where to go but the idea of someone wanting to visit him was too enticing.

'No, I'm here all day at the moment, like I said I'm off sick.'

'Great, I'll be round shortly.' Ray ended the call, as ever fully in control of all and every interaction Sean had ever had with him since he and Cathy had married fifteen years previously. Since their first meeting they had jostled for rank, boys in the playground elbowing each other to be top dog. Ray always seemed to hold a winning card up his disreputable sleeve, leaving Sean at an endless disadvantage, an unwillingly subservient pack member.

He sat now in the lounge. It had been an effort to leave the sanctuary of his bedroom den. It had become his world. Everywhere else was a monstrous undertaking of epic proportions. He was glad, whispering a quiet prayer of thanks, that the rest of the family weren't around to witness him sitting on the sofa trying to look at ease. Since when was he in the habit of praying, he wondered. The combination of sitting up and simultaneously wandering about the house exhausted him like a triathlon. The family were all in the habit of going shopping on a Saturday, the kids met their mates and Cathy liked browsing the fashion stores, a habit she'd had as a teenager. Her outings always included a purchase, sometimes modest, sometimes profligate which Sean had always suffered with cursory interest and a reference to his bank balance. When the front doorbell rang, he wearily hauled himself up wading through a fast-setting custard to answer it.

'Fuck me Sean, you look an effing state man,' Ray greeted him jovially nearly pushing him over as he barged over the threshold into the hall.

'Er come in, do,' said Sean desperately trying for an edge of sarcasm as he watched the back of his brother-in-law proceed without invitation into the lounge and plonk himself down on the sofa exactly where Sean had been sitting.

'So, what brings you here?' Sean leant on the edge of the doorway for support.

'Yes please, milk and two sugars' said Ray. Always apparently cheery, he had the knack of sharpening his words with an edge of threat: Sean not making him a cup of coffee might cost him dearly.

Sean, who wasn't in the habit of making anything for anyone but himself bristled but lacking the energy to resist found himself moving towards the kitchen wading through the now thickening sludge that used to be air. He hadn't managed to be this upright for weeks.

'Tea or coffee?' he called out as the kettle reached its boil and the effort of pulling the mugs from the cupboard brought him dangerously close. To collapse

'Either' came the unhelpful reply. Now he would have to decide. Ray had switched on the TV, muted the volume and was flipping through channels with the remote as if he was at home on his own sofa with his own remote. Sean staggered back in carrying the drinks. He'd considered whether a mug at a time was more effort than one trip with the weight of both, had lost an amount of liquid from each as a result, in an accidental libation to the carpet. Focused on a gymnastic display on the TV Ray took the proffered mug with brazen disregard and set it down slopping on the glass inlaid coffee table. The liquid, dirty brown as flood water pooled where glass and wood intersected.

'Nice arse,' he commented as the leotarded buttocks tensed pertly after a back flip.

Sean, emboldened by the achievement of making and carrying in a couple of cups of instant coffee picked up the remote and cancelled the image on the screen. This thug wasn't going to push him around in his own home. Ray put his feet up on the coffee table nudging the mug to spill some more of its contents onto the light pine surface.

'Aw sorry mate,' he sneered watching Sean retreat back into the kitchen for a wadge of kitchen roll. He gazed into the mug and grimaced, 'on half rations these days are we?'

The battle lost but the war still raging Sean sat down exhausted on the hard chair and stared at Ray who asked, 'How's Cathy?'

'Out shopping.'

'I didn't ask where, I asked how she was.' Ray tone now razor edged, any cheer absent.

'Well shopping usually makes her happy,' Sean tried to strike a lighter tone to the conversation, he was regretting letting him come here and needed to lie down. 'Tell me Ray, why are you here?'

'Well, Cathy's obviously concerned, she's got no idea what's got into you so I said I'd have a quiet word and as fortune would have it, I've a little proposition for you to fill in some of your spare time.'

'It's not spare time Ray, I'm off sick.'

'So, what does the doc say?'

'Well, she was pretty useless, but she did sign me off work for a month.'

'But you didn't get a diagnosis did you, so there's nothing really wrong with you is there? I know how it is you want a bit of paid holiday, time out from the daily grind.' Here Ray pinned him with a puckered stare as if assessing him for viability. 'You could help me out a bit, I've been let down. It'll at least get you out the house. Cathy needs a bit of time without you always under her feet. Everyone benefits.'

He managed to make it sound as if it had already been agreed so Sean, now flabbergasted, remained mute.

'You're alright to drive, aren't you? I just need a couple of deliveries picked up and dropped off. Simple stuff Sean, won't tax the brain cell too much and will bring in a bit extra for Cathy and the kids. Piece of piss really, look I'll let you know what time when and where. You won't let me down on this will you Sean? I'm sticking my neck out for you here, doing you a favour. It'd be upsetting for everyone to think you couldn't manage to return the good will of a close family member, eh?' He stared hard at Sean, steel knives flashing in eye sockets, 'I'll let myself out' and he walked to the door taking the remaining air with him.

☐

Belle opened her eyes and glanced at the alarm clock. She had allowed herself plenty of time to catch up on sleep before work, she didn't have to get up just yet. Despite not getting into bed before morning, she felt remarkably refreshed. Dancing did that for her. And there had been that unexpected frisson, an electrical boost of sexual excitement. She stretched out like a cat reviewing the details of the short but intense encounter and let herself nap. Instantly she was transported: A warm golden sun was gilding an orchard heavy with rosy, red apples. They shone, luminous. Above each fruit a pink bloom blushed, the blossom bordered by a garland of brilliant leaf green. A smiling woman appeared from the central trunk of the tree, shimmeringly unsolid, she wore a dress of blossom flowers that dazzled as she danced through the branches, impossibly flexible. 'You don't even need to eat the fruit!' she laughed as the whole vision burst into a cascading fountain of sparkling apples. As the shower reached her, she returned to consciousness.

'Wow what was that?' She jolted awake shocked by the sound of her own voice speaking aloud. Words blurting into the air seemed violent and snapped her back into the bedroom. She could hear the TV blaring away downstairs where her dad was watching afternoon sport. As the dream images subsided a sense of contentedness spread though her. Then, as if on cue the alarm clock started with its beeping tirade and she got up to shower and get ready for work.

☐

Feeling like an estate agent Karen had showed Matt the bedroom, bathroom, and kitchen, explaining their delicate plumbing idiosyncrasies. She had left him to unpack and 'settle in'. He stared around the chilly room. His nerves already jangled the kind voice calling up the stairs to ask if he wanted anything landed heavy and awkward, an intrusion, but at least more welcoming than the cold sloping walls.

'Sure, thanks.' Matt walked into the kitchen a little shyly. 'Er, I didn't get a chance to call in at the shops, it was a bit hectic packing up and…' his explanation tailed off as Karen looked at him sharply.

'Ok, let's get something straight. No excuses or explanations that include I would have but I didn't. If we're going to get along, you'll more than earn your keep and I wasn't expecting you to do a grocery shop when you're on the run for god's sake. There's plenty of time for you to go down to town and pick up provisions, all the time in the world in fact, but first things first, do you eat cheese on toast?'

Matt grinned. 'Yes, that's what we ate yesterday evening.'

'Oh, blimey, was it? And was that only yesterday? I must be losing it. Cheese on toast is one of my favourite things. Well, is it? I don't know…. living on your own it's hardly worth the effort to cook. I'll put something a bit more wholesome together.' Karen babbled nervously; she sounded like she was talking to herself, so Matt just nodded. He cleared his throat and glancing down at the table, shyly avoiding eye contact said, 'I can't tell you what this means to me, I mean thanks that you trust me like this, I won't let you down.'

'No, I don't believe you will,' she replied quietly. 'Want to get some logs in while I fix this haute cuisine? The log shed is round the back.'

Behind the cottage a mess of nettles and elder grew through and around a dilapidated fence. Rusting iron, dematerialising into lace, mildewed pieces of plastic gutter, old plant pots and a few cracked roof slates were thrown in a jumbled mix. A construction of wooden struts and corrugated tin sheeting rested against the stone wall of the cottage's back protecting a pile of split logs from the weather. They were stacked haphazardly. As he leant in to lift a few out Matt dislodged the precarious balance, narrowly escaping a wooden avalanche. He leapt out of the way sliding where he landed, the ground slick with mud, he juggled the logs managing to catch a couple. The sudden physicality of it made him laugh and retrieving the logs made a mental note to get the wood store organised, he'd look up how to stack them safely, it wasn't rocket science. The front door was permanently on the latch, so he pushed it open with his shoulder, arms piled high with his circus tricks. Next to the burner a dilapidated wicker basket sat, belly dilated with use. He dropped the wood into it. It creaked.

'You'll need to make some kindling,' Karen called from the kitchen, 'there's an axe under the shelf in the garden shed and a block for splitting it on.'

The only heating systems Matt had ever lived with were either gas or electricity activated by the flick of a switch. This wood burning lark appeared very labour intensive. He sighed under his breath and went back outside. Trees had only ever been scenery to him. Converting them to burn was a job. Even the wood he'd ever used for carpentry jobs was already sawn into workable plank sizes, it was as far from a tree as a vacuum-packed steak is from a cow. He went back out to what Karen had called the garden shed which was a little stone alcove immediately next to the living room wall and there was an axe and a big block of wood riven with the scars of multiple axe blows. An old vegetable crate with a peeling image of satsumas stapled to its side contained what looked like carpenters' off cuts, some had been split into smaller shards and he reckoned they must be the kindling. Balancing a largish piece on the block he brought the axe down and a sliver severed off at an awkward angle. Trying again with another strike he successfully split a piece that he thought would be about the right size to catch a flame but not too insubstantial. It was a satisfying feeling splitting the little bits off the bigger piece and he soon discovered that going against the grain of the wood didn't work. With each strike he felt something move through him, the exercise seeking to untangle all that had been held in his body over the recent weeks. The wood too had the story of its growth encoded in matter, it had its smell and its colour, it wasn't inert, it wasn't just a log with no history. He smiled to himself, enjoying the practical exertion of the task and the satisfying stack of kindling growing as a result and was almost sorry when Karen called him in to eat despite the growling in his stomach that wanted feeding.

'So where do you get your wood from?' He asked dusting splinters from his arms then washing his hands ready to eat.

'From my neighbour Joe who lives along the lane that way,' Karen waved a hand in a vague direction, 'I buy the logs from him, and because he sometimes does a bit of joinery work, when he has spare offcuts, he gives some to me.'

'That's a nice way to do it, like a whole way of life isn't it? I didn't realise when I first came out here.' Matt's voice trailed off wistfully.

'Indeed it is, and that's what you're going to learn if you're interested. You've got to be up for being out in the elements, on the earth, with the winds and rains and making the fire and of course tending to our lovely green friends.' Karen pointed outside to the garden and its border of trees and bushes that made up the hedge. Matt nodded, surprised to find that the idea of learning a different way of life not only kept his recent fears at bay but actively interested him. 'Yep, I think I'm going to like it.'

☐

Leaning on ramparts of the hill fort Alice sipped tea from her flask. She'd had a good day roaming on the hillside and breathing in the spacious view. The recent stresses were draining away through the soles of her feet into the generosity of the earth. She had stomped on browning bracken and close-cropped grass, the winter sky drooping mistily to kiss the hill's summit. Each footfall sent out a painful detail of children mistreated, born into stories of chaos. The weight of the stories had been threatening to drown her like too many pebbles in her pockets, but the majesty of the hill and the sky bathed her in resilience and now with the warm liquid washing down a very welcome sandwich, she felt once again complete and intact. However, when she reached the car park, ushered homewards by darkening clouds, the sight of Matt's car still parked there unsettled her. Her recovered composure was perhaps more fragile than she had supposed. An unwanted sense of responsibility for his welfare niggled at her, an itchy eczema under a collar: she wanted to scratch at it but knew it would flare up. The man was obviously a city dweller in townie's thin clothing, out here in twilight on his own with darkness falling soon, and he had behaved so strangely when they met. What if he intended to harm himself? She had attended enough workshops on the warning signs of mental health crises. Seeing the car apparently abandoned after hours had passed, the subliminal image of his head on the steering wheel clicked now into her conscious vision as if called on screen by a warning button. If he'd been out walking, she would have seen him at least from a distance on her hike, it was a clear horizon. There was nothing but the

113

occasional building for miles. He appeared to have vanished. She was the last person to have seen him alive, she saw the news footage, the police cordon tape as her mind whispered another story of tragedy into her unwilling ear. If she had but known to look behind her, there sheltered behind a stand of trees was a hedge bordering a garden surrounding a cottage from whose chimney a triumphant wisp of smoke emerged. Matt had just lit a fire in the wood burner, was sitting before it thrilled with warm satisfaction.

Alice drove off disgruntled by unbidden worry, her anxiety reactivated, she resented the intrusion into her carefully constructed peace, found blame and labelled him the cause.

After they had eaten Matt was washing up, delighting in the water heated by the back boiler of the wood burner. He called out to Karen. 'Do you know anywhere I could leave my car where it wasn't so obvious as the carpark?'

She was stroking a cat with one hand, looking at her phone in the other. 'What's this text from you, why do you want my bank details? If you were thinking of paying rent you can work for it, there's plenty to do here. You're a helpful guest not a lodger.'

'It's just I need to get most of the cash out of my account, I thought I could transfer it to yours.' Matt sounded disappointed.

'Very trusting of you but don't you think your nasty friends could trace it back to me, if they wanted?'

'They don't know we're connected; I shouldn't think they would think you were involved I could have just been buying a car off you or a holiday or something but if you don't want anything to do with it that's ok.' He'd been too complacent; his plan was unrealistic why had he thought she'd be willing?

'Let me think about it and I'll ask the neighbour about whether you could park off road on his track, he's got space.'

'Do you think he would mind?' Matt was now on high alert: no one else could be implicated in his disappearing act. Incongruous in this fairy tale cottage story he had tumbled into, the rectangle of green screen light lit up Karen's face. As if reading his mind Karen looked up and switched off the phone. Matt was standing awkwardly in the kitchen doorway.

"We can go round in the morning and ask; I'll see if he's around but do come and sit down by the fire for a while, you've had a hell of a day. We'll work out the money thing, it just needs some careful thought.'

Matt wasn't sure if he was being told off but slumped into the chair opposite Karen and stared through the charred glass behind which the flames danced intime to the winds playing the chimney like a flute.

It would be ok, it would be alright, it would work out. Somehow, it would work out. Karen was right. He was exhausted.

☐

Alice was properly irritated by the time she reached the greying streets of home. Streetlights poured an orange blaze onto concrete, stone, and brick. Windows flickered white, blue, black from TVs and computers pulsing through curtainless windows. She had failed to find a nearby parking spot and trudged now from a neighbouring street in sleety rain. The clouds of earlier had descended to earth to polish paving slabs with a wet sheen and passing head and tail lights caused a sparkle on the shop fronts as vehicles rushed past in pursuit of something else. Feeling weakened and annoyed with unwarranted concern, she turned the front door key and let herself in. She was going to have to call someone.

Whenever this tangled toxic empathy, an occupational hazard her mother insisted on calling it, got to her she was hard pressed to find an appropriate listener. Everyone had opinions. Some thought her mental health too fragile for the job, advising more regular adventure holidays, spa days or a new hair style. People would say smugly, you've got to leave your work at the office and smiled even more smugly that it was a metaphor when she pointed out that loads of people worked from home. She'd consulted doctors, supervisors, counsellors and even a psychotherapist. They had looked at her: down noses, across glasses, even angling ears directionally. They smiled sympathetically nodding with supposed comprehension but rarely had she ever felt that her inner mechanisms had been seen working and understood. And that was what she needed now. Someone who would listen without judgment, say just the right thing, be involved yet undemanding of her. She had never found a boy or girl friend who had come remotely close.

A solution wafted up from the onions frying in the pan as she cooked herself supper. Gus, of course, he might know more about that guy in the carpark. Perfect. Gus had seemed to like him, whatever his name was. A colleague of hers had gone out with him. That's how come she had ended up at the martial arts class in the first place. Her work mate had finished with him 'too predictable,' she'd said, but Alice liked his equanimity, they'd once spent an otherwise extremely boring works party chatting about the mistakes they had made and whether they had learned from them or not. It could have been a cringe worthy over personal conversation, but they had laughed like drains as they admitted horror story moments of foolishness. Shame she didn't fancy him. She'd call after she'd eaten. Saturday night he may not be home but just the possibility of contact lifted her mood.

□

The bed was cold. He had refused a hot water bottle thinking it a quaint childhood object regretting how useful it would have been between the almost frozen sheets. In the end he had put his socks back on and found a rarely worn beanie that he now felt intensely grateful for. Slowly warming up he was horrified to see his breath bloom into mist, a chill draught gathered all around him. This was a different kind of hard core from a city's tension and far from rural peace and quiet it was noisy outside with strange scuttling noises and screeching coming from all quarters.

Sheep coughed and shouted like men on a battlefield, owls hooted and tooted, something screamed and unknown fingers seemed to be scratching at the rooftiles. Despite it all he was soon fast asleep having barely slept the night before.

A man's voice startled him awake. It was ink dark. The room was freezing.

'Now son, yer canna rest here. We dunna want you ending up like yer old Pa now do we? There's a whole life waiting for yer. Yer munna head for the city like, that's where the streets are paved with gold me boy, go fetch yerself summat better, dunna wait here to be broken down like yer Pa. Since they took the land, we're naught but slaves.' A rake thin man was lying on a straw pallet in the corner of the room, a younger man kneeling at his side. The two figures glimmered, shifting in and out of focus.

Matt felt pinned down on his bed with crashing panic pounding his heart. It took long moments to subside as he gradually remembered where he was and the presence in the room waned as he tried to concentrate his mind on his shivering body as if that would bring him back to himself, away from the strange scene. He was so totally confused he pulled the quilt over his head and took a long slow breath. As if something was slipping or had tripped a circuitry, a stack of dominoes was collapsing, there was no familiar pattern. He struggled to rearrange pieces from the wrecked perceptual jumble and found he had no coordination. Pushing back the covers again he stared up at the unfamiliar ceiling and a convulsion exploded from his chest. There was no holding this heaving down and so finally he didn't try. Clutching the pillow into his face he gave in to an enormous force. Years of accumulation collapsed into the stiletto heel of this moment, he sobbed as if the earth was quaking, and a tidal wave surged in response, whoever he was floated unanchored.

It was after dawn before hollowed out he slept again in a cavernous slumber. Until there came a tap at the door. It creaked open and Karen's head poked into the room. 'Cuppa? I wasn't sure whether to wake you, but it's gone eleven and Joe is expecting us.' No sequential understanding followed. Instead, Matt grunted incoherently as Karen set down a cup of steaming liquid on the little table. 'I'll leave you to it.'

When he finally woke again it was twilight and despite still feeling as if a stranger had stepped into his skin he at least knew where he was and that he had slept a long time and was in that woman Karen's house. He heard radio noise billowing up from the downstairs room and dragged himself out of bed. He was busting for a pee. Down the narrow stairs there was no sign of a soul all the way through the living room to the toilet. No cat, no human other than the radio's burbling and after relieving himself in the freezing bathroom he went and sat by the fire which was chuntering away giving out the only light in the fast-darkening room. The front door flung open suddenly, a blast of chill air flew in, and Karen appeared with a stack of logs in her arms, the cat at her legs. Matt stiffened and started to get up.

'Relax,' she said depositing the logs then walking into the kitchen. Noises of chopping and sizzling soon followed and he continued sitting, staring into the flames unable to galvanise into action. Only slowly, as if emerging from a deep-sea dive, pausing to allow for decompression to avoid the bends, did Matt began to steady himself and arrive back fully present in the room that was fast becoming familiar. The big black cat slunk towards him, carefully placed paws on his thighs then leapt soundlessly onto his lap. The cat's amber eyes looked inscrutably into his own, his warm weight and soft fur rippling as he purred in satisfaction. Matt had never had a pet. Now with the contented feline rumbling and the gentle hiss and phut of the fire he could allow a memory of the dramatic intensity of the night. Alongside fear was the sense that something was opening up in him and Matt intuitively knew that this was exactly what he needed, to break apart some self-imposed barriers, to see beyond the apparent, to feel stuff. That first kung fu class had cracked a façade, the radical departure from his flat had swung the sledgehammer. Somewhere in him he was willing the gentle presence of his mum to guide him. Well maybe not her exactly, but he was ready to trust to a knowing influence that wouldn't allow him to keep going down the wrong track.

Karen entered the room bringing a hot dish from the kitchen and set it on the table. 'Tadaa!' she announced, 'cottage pie, I haven't made one in years but to celebrate your great escape here it is. And don't think I'll be cooking every night, it's a special occasion.' She'd put her oven gloved-hands on hips and bowed.

Matt smiled, mumbling 'sleeping the day away like that I blew all the arrangements, I…' Karen interrupted. 'Eat first, it's all fine we can visit Joe later in the week, no problem.'

And she ladled out a steaming portion of golden crusted pie that smelled like all the nourishment he had ever longed for. He was starving.

Chapter thirteen

Alice had been correct in thinking that Gus would be busy the day before. By the time he got back to her she felt very distanced from the hillside drama. Still, it was good to hear his voice and after the preliminary how's it going, she launched straight into why she had rung.

'What do you know about the guy in your class, razored hair, athletic build, bit of a swagger, maybe my age, mart, mick, think it began with an M…'

'Matt?' Gus sounded cautious, 'is this official stuff?'

'No nothing like that, it's just I bumped into him yesterday.'

'And?' Alice could hear a touch of humour in his voice now as if Gus thought she was interested in him as a romantic prospect.

'Behave. I took myself off to a hill for a stomp, stuff at work's been getting me down and I met him in the carpark there looking and acting properly stressed, I mean head in hands weird and distracted.'

'Maybe he needed a bit of time out too,' said Gus cautious but interested.

'Well, I guess that's what I thought except that come the evening on my way back his car was still parked there, it was getting dark and ready to rain. There was no sign of him anywhere out on the hill and it's not like there's many places to detour to and he didn't strike me like a country kind of person, I mean he was wearing trainers and jeans, no waterproofs or anything and he really seemed out of sorts, we were both shocked to meet in such an out of the way place…' Alice's explanation trailed off uncertainly.

'Hmm yeah does sound a bit unlikely, I mean I don't really know him, he's only been to class a couple of times, but I thought he showed promise. He seemed quite shy or not very sociable or something. Leave it with me, I think I've got his number.'

'Or a bit shady and dodgy,' Alice added.

'Maybe, but I like him anyway, shady, dodgy, or not, there's something interesting about him, more than meets the eye. Mind you don't get jaded and let your work nose cloud your judgment, we've all got our shadows.' Gus had a way of saying it straight without causing offence. 'I'll try and contact him and let you know when he tells me about how he was in training for a through the night triathlon in civvies.' Gus laughed. 'Are you coming to class on Thursday? I'll text you when I hear, or see you there, in the meantime try not to worry there's probably some very boring explanation though I agree it's a bit unusual.'

Alice was happy to be reassured, she'd almost forgotten how rattled she had been. They left the subject of Matt wherever he might be and chatted about other things. After the call Gus checked his contacts. Quietly congratulating his organisational skills, he found Matt in the list of students. He rang the number and when it went to answer machine clicked off without leaving a voice message. Instead, he texted a friendly note.

☐

Another text pinged into Sean's phone late. He'd managed an evening in front of the TV with Cathy though they hadn't spoken much. The kids were in their rooms, occasional exclamations audible through the ceiling and Cathy was mostly on her phone now and then passing comment on some actor's looks or outfits. For his part Sean wasn't following the story line, the series of moving images stupefied his dulled senses with the anaesthesia of constant movement as his wearied brain tried to resolve the pixels into something recognisable. It was exhausting and he wasn't sure if he'd been snoring. He checked the message after turning off the TV.

Tomorrow 11am, be ready I'll show you the ropes.

Sean sighed and rubbed forehead and face as if trying to erase his features.

'You alright?' asked Cathy disinterested and on her way to bed.

'Just Ray on my back, wants me to do him a favour tomorrow. I just don't think I'm up to it.'

Cathy looked at him, swamped by irritation.

'Sean, you're going to have to get out there sometime, Ray's only trying to help. Why don't you try it?' And when that met a blank, 'for me?' A sweet smile. Or was it threatening, faked? Sean no longer knew. But he did know he was overruled and, shocked by how quickly the balance of power had swung, pushed himself up from the indented sofa and meekly murmured ok. If he was having to go out in the morning, he'd better get some sleep if that was what the unrefreshing muffled unconsciousness was called.

☐

A cold drizzle accompanied dawn. The hill was in cloud. Three days clear of any weed and more sleep than he'd known for years Matt woke early. Silence pounded an inaudible heartbeat in the rest of the cottage telling him Karen was still sleeping. He had no idea what time it was, not yet fully light. He didn't want to switch on the lamp but instead drew the curtains and peered out through the murky damp. He didn't want to switch on his phone either. The longer he kept it switched off the further away any unwelcome messages would be, the longer it stayed dormant the better. Matt felt uneasy in the quiet of the room as if the man's voice could penetrate the atmosphere. He got out of bed and dressed hurriedly. Downstairs the cats wound themselves around his legs insinuating it was breakfast time, 'sorry' he whispered, 'I don't know where she keeps your grub,' then he went outside.

Walking into the garden, dripping trees splattering sounds, the birdsong was sparse and the ground slippery. Reaching the rickety gate, he went through it and out onto the common. Cropped grass, thistle and nettle huddled close to the ground along with the rotting remains of various fungi melting back into where they had sprung from. Swathes of bracken shone conker coloured with moisture, dew wet webs were strung upon the gorse. The murky grey from the window looked very different once you were in it and a slight breeze revealed momentary scenes emerging across the valley: wispy dreams of clarity emanating from a sodden sponge. He took a deep lungful of air and started coughing, all the sludge of smoking loosening, dredged then spat out as phlegm. He started to jog up hill to gain even more of a view. Pounding through the drizzle it seemed to part, encouraging him onwards. He felt himself speed up, arms joining the race, pumping in time with legs as foot bounced on turf and heart and lungs synchronised. The rain permeated his clothing and settled on the exposed skin of face, hands and hair and he was soon as wet as if he'd taken a shower. Exhilarated, he ran on. In the distance the land was bumpy where a circular rampart crowned the horizon. He decided to head for it settling into a sustainable pace. As he covered the ground there was not a soul in sight, he felt entirely alone in the world as if he himself was the world. He was the large sky, the majestic slopes of hill, the movement of limbs, the outlines of trees, the cushioning earth, the inhale of breath, everything was part of him and not him at the same time. A final push up to a gap in the ramparts and he was in the hill fort. Hands on knees he leant forward to steady his breath sweating and thrilled by the achievement of arrival.

In the distance a dog walker was being tugged along by a straining puppy, water skiing along the rampart. Matt watched as the little dog broke free and raced across the distance between them covering ground with the agility of a deer whilst the dog walker shrieked useless commands and stumbled along behind out of breath and puffing. Matt patted the dog's silky head as it leapt up muddying the thighs of his soaking jeans. Of the same exuberant energy, they played a dodging game until the owner arrived. 'Sorry!' He gasped, red faced, 'he'll be the death of me!'

'No worries,' said Matt preparing to run off before the walker could start chatting, 'nice dog.'

'You'd be welcome to him if you like, got too much energy for me, I got saddled with him.'

Matt was already jogging away before he registered the man's words, he was heading for the opposite banks of the ancient monument as 'No! Heel! Down!' echoed with diminishing volume.

By the time he reached the cottage, the mizzle had lightened to a mere atomising spray, but he was sodden inside and out, the denim of his jeans a cold and restrictive force.

Was there even a shower here? At least the front door was still on the latch, he hadn't thought of that before letting himself out earlier.

Inside the cottage was warm with the smell of toast and coffee.

'Ah there you are, want a brew?' Karen was reading a book with a half-finished cafetiere and the remnants of toast in front of her on the table. 'Goodness you're soaked and filthy, is it still raining?'

'Could I have a shower? Is there a shower?'

'You weren't paying attention on your guided tour yes there's a shower, help yourself and don't think you have to ask every time you want a wash, I'd much prefer you washed than didn't.' She laughed.

Matt went to retrieve his washbag and towel from the bin bag under the bed, catching a whiff of the flat he had left behind emanating from it. Far from evoking any nostalgia he found the musty smell nauseating; it communicated passive smoking infiltrated with an imprisoned fetid loneliness. He opened the bedroom window and flapped the towel about outside.

Under the shower was total refreshment. His skin, red from exertion felt purified. The pile of sodden garments lay in a heap on the floor. He'd have to ask about laundry as well. How long could this generosity last? Caught between gratitude and awkwardness at the loss of autonomy he understood just how important it was going to be for him to make himself useful. After breakfast and instruction on how to use the washing machine he asked Karen for a list of jobs she would like him to do, eager to eliminate any fear on her part that he was a free loader and wouldn't prove himself worthy of her benevolence. He could surprise her with restacking the precariously balanced log store. She hadn't put that on the list. The dense grey lifted; he was outside again, on a mission.

In the corner of the wood store, a decaying tarp was scrunched up like litter, he hauled it out and laid it on the ground. With both hands he was grabbing logs from the ramshackle pile chucking them down and warming once again to the rhythm and satisfaction of the simple physical task.

He then replaced them, log by log, stacking each in turn like bricks in a wall except they weren't so uniformly shaped. It was something of a puzzle to balance them as effectively as a stack of alligators so that each successive storey settled evenly on the one beneath. It didn't take him long and he stood back proudly surveying the tidy pile, shook out the tarp, folding and rolling it into a neat bundle that fitted into the remaining space. The young tabby cat sat perched on a fence post, tail neatly wrapping her paws and blinking approval. He stopped to stroke her head and she arched a rippling back and leapt down.

Next job the gate. That was on the list along with gutters, paving slabs, pruning, path clearing, fencing and did he think he could manage a bit of roofing? In no particular order. These was just the things that had flown from Karen's head. She had captured them on a little chalk board that hung on the kitchen wall. He in turn could cross them off, setting them free with a sleeve or a dampened finger as they each were mended. She had said that tools were somewhere in the garden shed but it was rammed so full he decided the simplest thing was to empty it all out and reorganise, he didn't want to keep wasting time playing hide and seek. He liked the feeling that one thing led to another; it soothed the need to keep thinking ahead, an invisible sequence was leading him around the garden paths, dropping clues to an imminent future.

Emptying the shed he found paint pots and pegs, old crockery, and rusting chicken wire, a broken umbrella, snow shovel and a bag stuffed full of other old bags among other things vying for space on a set of rickety shelves. Why did she keep all this stuff? Eventually he unearthed an old toolbox from under a stack of deconstructed cardboard boxes. Its blue metal veneer was scratched and rust worn as a shipwreck, and the hinged lid didn't want to open without persuasion, creaking when it did like an arthritic joint. Inside it however, Matt found himself absorbed by a treasure trove of useful tools kept in remarkably good condition. Hammer, pliers, screwdrivers, alen keys, boxes of screws and nails, hacksaws, wire clippers, wood glue and oil and somethings he didn't recognise but that looked useful.

Karen appeared blocking the light through the door frame. 'Where did you get all these from?' He realised he sounded incredulous.

'A woman's toolbox is a thing of beauty is it not?' She teased, 'I can't take full credit. The neighbour I told you about, Joseph, he put it together for me when I first came here and to be honest, I'm not as handy as I'd like to be which is why I appreciate your help here. Gardening is my thing. The rest of it is a bit overwhelming.'

'But what about your landlord, why doesn't he fix stuff?'

'He's an old man now and besides the rent is so reasonable I don't like to make demands or else his family could just kick me out, they're itching to get their hands on the place, so we want him alive as long as possible, not worn out by too many demands of endless maintenance.'

Matt made a face. In his world the landlord fixed things in exchange for the rent, otherwise no rent. But this wasn't his world.

'Is there a bigger saw anywhere? And timber? The gate needs a piece replacing.'

'I doubt it, but that's the perfect reason to visit Joe and you can ask him if he's alright for you to park your car there.'

Shit, he'd forgotten about the car.

'Let's go down there now. It's probably best to move it as soon as possible, Joe said he'd be around.'

Matt's skimpy coat was still soaked but he put it on anyway to go visiting, woefully aware that high street fashion didn't work so well with wind and rain and little shelter. Concrete stored warmth, acted as a barricade. Tarmac and paving slabs kept trainers clean. His were now stained from the red earth of the run. At least the high hedges provided some cover from the chilly breeze that hit them as they rounded the corner beyond the carpark where Matt's car sat as if abandoned. A little further along the lane they turned onto a track towards a yard bordered by a straggling hedge of rose, hawthorn, hazel and elder. At the point where the track opened into the wider space of the yard was a huge pile of wood. It looked like someone had just felled a forest and dumped it there. Behind the woodpile was a scrubby potholed yard with a couple of vehicles and a trailer parked up. Neither vehicle looked particularly well maintained: one was dented and scratched and the other covered in bird droppings. A telephone wire crossed the yard from a post on the lane and was fixed to the side of a stone cottage which flanked the yard. Matt wondered if he even wanted to leave his car here. His car, his security, his statement of success, what if someone tipped a lorry load of tree trunks on it?

'Hi Joseph!' Karen called.

Out from the faded red front door loped a man of indeterminate age wiping his hands on a piece of rag that he retrieved from the pocket of his overalls. His cap shaded deep blue eyes that quietly took in the visitors.

'Hello Karen, how are you?' and giving her a hug looked at Matt, 'and who's this young un?'

'Joe, this is Matt he's staying with me for a while, giving me a hand with stuff.'

'I'm glad to hear it.' His voice had the burr of a regional accent that Matt didn't recognise. He extended a hand scarred solid with years of work, fingernails scuffed, palm rough yet remarkably warm, 'Pleased to meet you.

It was impossible to tell what he was thinking. Matt felt as if he was being scanned, impersonal but not unfriendly.

'We were wondering if Matt could park his car up here. We don't want it left too long in the carpark, looks abandoned, or someone might spot it.' Matt shot Karen a warning glare, too much information.

'Sure, no problem. 'Joe was inscrutable. 'But you'll have to get a ticket and payment is a hand with some log splitting.'

'Ah right,' Matt hesitated. 'Yeah, be happy to but my only experience is making a bit of kindling.' Matt looked sheepish; Joe grinned like a wolf.

'You haven't split logs, you haven't lived, we need to shift this pile anyway so's you can get your car in, and I can get my van out. It got dropped off when I wasn't here. Someone was in a hurry.' Despite the inconvenience Joe didn't appear to be at all bothered.

'Good to have some young blood around, I can be foreman.' Joe smiled at his own joke. 'And can you handle a chainsaw?'

'Not yet but I reckon if you showed me, I could learn.'

'That's what I like to hear.' Joe turned and it was clear he expected Matt to follow.

'Well, I'll see you back at the cottage later then,' said Karen feeling surplus to requirements, 'I've got things to do too,' and she left the two men walking across the yard, half wondering if it might be more fun to hang around here with them. But as she turned to go, she saw the two men looking like peas in a pod, striding away into the workshop.

Chapter fourteen

'The first and most important thing to know about splitting logs is not to hit yourself,' explained Joe, 'that is your legs or feet, the only other damage would be to your skull if the head of the splitter flies off on the upswing and you don't know where it's going to come down.' Joe smiled, eyes twinkling with mischief, 'in that eventuality just stand still, hold your breath and close your eyes and prepare to meet your maker while you wait for the impact,' he looked at Matt, 'but this isn't going to happen because I've got a new state of the art splitter.'

'Did that happen to you?' Matt was fully reined into the intrigue.

'I did have that happen twice in fact with the old wooden shafts but not the impact bit, I was lucky, nine lives see. And it won't happen with this new Norwegian beauty.' They had reached a working station where a sawhorse and chopping block crisscrossed with wedged indentations stood amidst a pile of damp sawdust. Joe ducked into his workshop and emerged proudly displaying the splitter which looked to Matt like a giant long handled axe. 'To be fair,' he said, 'whatever you're working with you should check it first, you know what they say about workmen and their tools.'

Matt wasn't sure he did but thought it best to stay quiet since Joe was clearly on a roll.

'The thing about wood is its still alive even when its chopped down and machined into planks. The life story is there in the markings, the knots and the rings of growth. Can you handle that stump? Better to take it over to the pile than make extra work for ourselves. Let the dog see the rabbit.'

He went back to fetch the chainsaw and sawhorse and chucking Matt a pair of ancient ear defenders deftly sliced up some of the long trunks, angling the rotating blade as expertly as a chef dicing vegetables. When there was a good heap, and the original pile was almost halved he shut off the whining machine.

'That's the noisy bit done. I couldn't hear myself think!'

Picking up a section of log the width of a middle-aged tree he balanced it on the splitting block.

'To start you off you want a straight grain no knots piece. It's easier to split. And easy is right.'

He raised the splitter and with what looked like a vertical golfer's swing let the splitter fall to crack the log in half.

Handing the tool to Matt he said, 'You've got to mean it when you bring it down, show it who's boss.'

Matt took up a stance lifted the splitter above his head and let it fall. On impact it bounced off, toppling the piece onto the floor. Annoyed he went to retrieve it, but Joe was there first. 'I'll be your putter onner,' and he balanced it back on the block.

This time Matt took up a posture and remembered the Kung Fu class. He let the splitter fall and felt the gravity and momentum meet in the action. The log gave way like a knife through butter. He laughed in satisfaction. The two men set up a working rhythm and barring a couple of duff swings Matt had demolished the pile in record time.

'I'm impressed, hat's off to you,' said Joe, pushing the cap back off his forehead to wipe the sweat from his brow and scratch his head. 'I always say you get warm three times with wood, hauling it, splitting it and burning it. And it's good to work up an honest sweat. Cuppa? And then chainsaw lesson?'

Sometimes the depth of simple joy is impossible to articulate, ungraspable it eludes description. Working alongside this man Matt was at ease and enjoying himself. It wasn't simply that it was an entirely new experience to be so immediately accepted, nor the pleasure of finding a satisfying task that was devoid of any complexity or simply the sense that he was in the presence of someone who knew a lot about a lot of things but wasn't trying to prove anything. The man could have been his dad or possibly grandad? He was fit but judging by his skin and grizzled silver hair he could even have been well past retirement age. He simply didn't compare to any of the men Matt had ever encountered. He liked him and felt he was liked in return. There was security in that. And promise. It was balm. Perhaps for the first time he felt that glimmer of hope that finally he might get on the right path and that the flight from the city wasn't only necessary to get him out of the prison of a situation but was going to free him inside.

◻

Sean made sure he was showered and dressed in good time. He had drunk an extra cup of coffee in the vain hope that the caffeine would perk him up. He was resting on the sofa awkwardly anticipating Ray's arrival. As before he was on his own in the house.

As accurately as a Swiss train, Ray's Alfa Romeo swung into the drive when the numbers on Sean's phone clock clicked to 1100. He opened the front door.

'We'll go in yours.' Ray gave the command and when Sean faltered, a look so venomous had him automatically turning to fetch the car keys from the little hook above the kitchen counter.

'I haven't driven for a while,' he mumbled.

'It's like riding a bike' said Ray unsympathetically, 'no time to lose, let's go' and he hustled Sean out of his own front door and into his family saloon.

Back in the driving seat Sean found he could in fact operate the car as Ray barked directions which lead them out of the city.

'Where are we going exactly?' asked Sean, gazing at the fuel gauge. In reply Ray gave him the what3words and postcode.

I meant how far in terms of petrol use.' Sean tried a hint of sarcasm.

Ray leaned over and looked at the dials. 'You should have enough in there,' he said unhelpfully. 'The less you know about it the better. The less questions you ask the more successful you'll be. Only ask on a strictly need to know basis.

When you do this alone, you'll receive the details by text, time and coordinates. Simply put them into your maps app and follow the instructions.' Patronising would be to compliment Ray's tone. 'The guy we're meeting today will hand you a package and you bring it back and that's it. Don't worry you'll receive a cut, it'll be worth your while.'

'But I don't need this, I'm still on sick pay, I'll be back at work when I'm a bit better.' Any residual buoyancy in Sean was deflating now, he was flailing about trying to keep his head above water.

'You may, you may not. Either way this will tide you over and you're returning a favour after all.'

Sean was struggling to remember what favour. He kept eyes staring forward through the windscreen to avoid the moving targets that bobbed past while his lungs seemed to be filling with water. Bigger roads led to lesser ones, and soon they were driving down rural country lanes. High hedges on banks of rock and earth created near tunnels where trees' twig fingers interlaced overhead. They were climbing up a steep bank when Ray broke the silence.

'We're getting close, it's a layby just up here on the left.'

Rounding a corner there was a dark hatchback idling up ahead, its red brake lights jewelling the lane, a faint wisp of exhaust scenting the air.

'Pull in behind him.' Sean obeyed, gulping for air.

Ray went to the driver's door window, had a few words. The driver leaned over to retrieve something from the passenger footwell then pushed himself out from the car seat. As he unfolded his bulk, a spray of crisp crumbs bounced off a large belly. He wiped an oily moustache with the back of a gold ringed fist and strolled towards Ray.

'Mr Saunders,' he introduced himself. 'Keep talk to a minimum, be on time and you'll be fine.' With that he practically threw a brick sized package into Sean's lap, turned and swaggered away.

'Let's go,' said Ray when the other car had pulled into the lane.

At the top of the hill the lane opened out into a small carpark. Mr Saunders had stopped, indicator winking. 'What now?' said Ray impatiently. He got out again and led Ray to a blue hatchback parked in the corner of the otherwise empty space. The whine of machinery was audible through the open door.

Sean saw Ray's expression change and watched as he took out his phone and snapped the reg plate. They were soon on their way again after Ray issued a clipped instruction to get going.

It was not until they were approaching the city that Sean ventured conversation.' What was that all about back there?'

'Don't you worry your not so pretty head about it. What did I say about asking questions?' But Ray couldn't resist bragging. 'I just want to get someone to check on that number plate for me, find out who owns it.'

'I wouldn't have thought that kind of information is available to any tom, dick or harry' said Sean innocently.

'Sean, Sean, any kind of information is readily available if you know who to ask, besides, my name is Ray not any of those other bastards.' He smiled a nasty smile and that shut Sean up. Neither man spoke again until Ray gave directions to an industrial estate on the western edge of the city.

'This is where you'll be depositing what you pick up.'

Sean dutifully swung the car into the tarmacked carpark space of a plumbing supplies warehouse and followed Ray to a door next to the reception which was fitted with a secure drop box.

'Simply post it in here and bob's your uncle, couldn't be simpler, like I said, a piece of piss. Let's get back to yours now Sean so I can pick up my car, I've another appointment to get to.'

'Listen Ray, I was happy to help you out here today,' Sean lied, 'but I'm not looking for a job. I don't want to be involved with whatever this is. As soon as I feel well enough, I'll be back at work. I'm constantly wiped out these days, I don't need any extra pressure.'

The air turned icy. Ray, all pretence absent, fixed him with a freezing glare.

'Sean, I didn't want to have to spell it out, but I can see you haven't fully comprehended. Your options are narrowing as we speak, I know people who will start complaints procedures, you made some enemies back at work. I need someone to help me out for a while. You're not ready to go back yet, you told me so yourself. Cathy asked me to encourage you to start doing something, she's at her wits end and losing patience with you. If you want to return to work, why wouldn't you want to help? Consequences Sean there are always consequences. Sometimes there are cracks you simply don't want to fall through. Don't disappoint me. It's a generous offer I've made. A little gratitude wouldn't go amiss. Now drive. I have another appointment.'

Sean drove.

When they arrived back home Ray unbuckled his seat belt and slapped Sean on the shoulder. 'I hope we understand each other' he said with finality, decanting himself from one vehicle to the other and driving away. Sean continued to sit there, trying to arrange the experience into some acceptable interpretation. He remembered watching a cat torment a little shrew. Strange how he should recall that just now. His liver tried in vain to squirt out the build-up of bile. However hard he tried he couldn't digest this latest turn of events; he'd never managed to stomach his unsavoury brother-in-law at the best of times but now he wanted to vomit.

☐

By the descent of evening, they had finished processing the entire wood pile and were sat in Joe's kitchen having a beer to celebrate.

'Nicely done Matt, thanks for your help, you can park your car up now.' Joe held up his bottle in cheers. Matt did too and they clinked.

'You have to make eye contact,' said Joe.

'You what?'

'Make eye contact when you do cheers,' Joe held up the bottle and clinked it again, this time Matt looked up into Joe's eyes and they smiled at each other.

'Can I ask you something Joe?'

'Fire away.'

'Do you believe in ghosts?'

Joe took a breath. 'Quite simply,' he said 'yes. I can tell that what you're asking is whether something you've had happen is real. This world we can see is by no means all there is.' He slapped the table with an open palm. 'Anyone who tells you otherwise has themselves been brainwashed. Messages from beyond the grave are usually to let you know something is unquiet. There's a horrible lot of dishonesty and corruption in this world, but equally extraordinary gifts and loving abundance. It all depends on how you take notice and choose to live. Here he tapped his heart. 'I should know, I lived as a thief for a couple of years when I was a young man. I mean I used to look through the quarter inch plate glass window and see the food you could buy if you had money and if you didn't you could starve, and I thought that was unfair. Still do really. It was the injustice, that's what gave me the impetus to start shop lifting, me and a friend, we did it together. It wasn't that I wanted to rob anyone, it was that everything seemed dishonest to me so why shouldn't I be too. But things didn't go too well for me taking like that. In the end the reason why I stopped was because I imagined a small shop keeper who one day notices something's missing, knows nobody bought it so then everybody who comes into the shop is under suspicion, is a potential thief so that shop keeper loses their trust in human beings in general and besides all the other book balancing that's what's the worst thing wrong with stealing, it creates its own unfairness.'

Matt was quiet, 'didn't you have any family then?'

'I loved my mum, but she had married a man who didn't like me, well to be fair I wasn't that keen on him either, so I'd left home as soon as I could, I never knew my own father.'

'Me neither,' said Matt with companionable sympathy.

'It took me a while to find what it was I liked doing that could earn me a living. I used to think a job was something you weren't supposed to enjoy and that's why they paid you for it. Nobody ever told me you could love what you do. But at least I found out. I'm grateful for that.'

'Was that working with wood?'

'Yep. I like it because it's clean and the variety of timber and the variety of things you can make with it is limitless and you don't have to be part of a big organisation to get on with it. And that's where I discovered the world of spirits and ghosts too. The forest is full of them. Human and otherwise. And peoples' houses. But that my friend is a whole other story.'

They had finished their beer and Joe suddenly looked tired. Matt got up to go.

'Would you be able to help me fix Karen's gate; I don't mean do it but help me work out the best way?'

'I will. Do a drawing of it and I'll show you what I would do. Bring it round when you bring the car. I'm here all day tomorrow.'

'Thanks Joe, it's been a great day.'

'Right on Matt and give my regards to Karen, she's a very nice woman.'

'I will, she is doing me a massive favour.' And he left wondering if Joe was perhaps a bit sweet on her. Later that evening he finally turned on his phone. The only message that caught his attention and demanded a response was one from Gus.

Hey mate, alice from class said she saw you out at some remote country place a bit concerned later when your car still parked there. just checking you ok and coming to class Thursday? let me know.

A flare of irritation shot through him. Why did Alice need to make something of it? Nosy or what? Torn between annoyance at the interference, and a kind of seeping warmth from the existence of care and concern that he wasn't as disappeared as he'd like to be, he composed a reply that he hoped would strike a friendly but non-committal tone:

All good ta, just taking time out of town a while sorry not there thursday. cheers matt.

Thankfully he could move the car tomorrow and finally get off the radar. Was it ever possible to completely disappear? Out here on this hill in the supposed middle of nowhere he felt himself much more visible than he had ever been. Here he had also found two friends who were ready to accept him and perhaps more importantly to whom he could be useful, and it had all come about so effortlessly. He didn't care they were years older than him. Powered by a pulse that was both exciting and novel he was also frightened that it could all too easily shatter and cease. These were the thoughts that slid wearily from him before he dropped off to sleep, limbs exhausted from physical labour but comforted by wrapping themselves around the now familiar hot water bottle.

Karen sat downstairs by the fire with one cat on her lap, the other delicately curled in a furry spiral. She was grappling with something like the irritation of an intermittent fly or tiny splinter that when pressed sends a sharp pain but defies extraction. It was small enough to want to ignore but persistent enough that she couldn't. Matt had returned elated from the day's work with Joe. He'd cooked up a dish which they'd eaten chatting about working with wood and it had all been friendly and companionable. There was nothing to complain of in that. But now, what was it made her want to weep? As she sat quietly knowing that Matt would be safely asleep, a stab of jealousy invaded her privacy. The loss of her son to his father loomed, an unprocessed grief, a festering repetition. Matt wasn't James and Joe wasn't anything like Bill, but still this feeling of being marginalised persisted. She felt ashamed to admit that potentially losing Matt to Joe, crazy though that seemed, wounded her. She felt pathetically sorry for herself, supposing that when the gates of solitude open a flood of disturbing relational possibilities start pouring in. She wasn't convinced it was entirely to her liking. Wasn't it far better to have things under control and organised as you liked them. The rest of it seemed prone to get messy. She was tempted to open a bottle of wine, she hadn't drunk at supper because Matt said he'd just had a beer, and she resisted now, hearing a small persistent voice reminding her to ride this moment out, to feel it properly so that it didn't become another ghost echoing pain, echoing disillusion, echoing loss of love. She wept instead; tears saturated with stress hormones poured dammed up tension onto the accommodating black fur of the cat rumbling purred encouragement. Viewed through droplets of grief her living room melted, solidity disintegrating as her chest heaved and subsided, an ocean surging, draining into a hiss of shingles upon a refreshed shore. A handful of damp tissues later she felt herself restored enough to go quietly up to bed.

Chapter fifteen

How was it that everyone was expected to stay longer than they were paid for? That the workload exceeded the time available was clear but that the service managers somehow created an illusion the workers were falling short and therefore had to make up time, that was the killer. It was the ultimate definition of stress, never being able to complete a task because it was simply impossible. And all this in highly charged, emotionally traumatic situations resulted in pure toxic overload. Her day had involved three routine assessments of child protection, an emergency case conference of indescribable sordidness, a missed lunch break covering for a sick colleague and an afternoon typing up reports. Her phone had pinged with a text from Gus.

Just to let you know I heard back from Matt. all ok, he's taking time out.xx

Well bully for him Alice thought bitterly, resenting the wasted care. She felt an active dislike rising that caused her mouth to screw up in a sour purse and her eyes, heavily screen weary, to harden and narrow. What a wanker. She really needed to learn to turn off her over responsible sense of duty for useless wasters.

Politely she replied, *Thanks for letting me know.*

Glancing at the time she saw she was way overdue getting home, drained the last of a cold cup of coffee and shrugging on her jacket stomped out of the office.

A group of friends were going to the cinema that evening to see a new film. She'd also said she'd talk to another girlfriend from college who had recently had a baby and was struggling with lack of sleep, her folks wanted a catch up, but if she stayed in and didn't talk to anyone, she could finish off the backlog of reports. Dismally that last option was the most appealing. A couple of seagulls squawked overhead. They had followed the river inland to scavenge at the city's dump and beady eyed saw her back bowed against the dark evening.

Thanks mate. Ray clicked off from the phone and scratched his stubbling chin. It was as they'd thought. It was his car. Question was what was it doing there? A vague memory surfaced as he sipped his scotch. *Someone's living up there, it's not safe.* He liked to think of himself as something of a sleuth, he needed to be for effective manipulation he thought smiling to himself. But this, it was curious. The guy falls off the edge of the planet after refusing them their offer, always so dependable, reliable, easy. Multiple scenarios played in Ray's mind. Perhaps their work had already been done for them, he grinned maliciously. The lad wouldn't be fool enough to leave a vehicle out there for them to find, or would he? They'd already been round to the flat, the letting agents knew he'd gone, his bank account hadn't been touched since a cash withdrawal a couple of days ago. He himself had dematerialised but his motor was still very much solid matter. How anyone could be living up there was beyond him, they must live in a ditch somewhere there was no drive or gateway, how the hell could you get to such a place without a vehicle? Flummoxed but intrigued he started texting. He'd send Sean over to have a look about. The illuminated rectangle shuddered in the darkened bedroom. Despite his exhaustion Sean fumbled for it and read the instruction. If he'd had any energy, it might have plummeted further. As it was the sewers were already full of him, drained like a hung carcass in an abattoir. All he was aware of was the dread of having to exert himself and a dark cave of loathing for the man making him. The noises of family life droned on behind the walls isolating him further into his malevolent cocoon, he feared his own liquification. He would go sometime tomorrow. If he stayed here, he feared he might finally drown.

'It's you,' Gus said simply, placing the bottle on the counter and grinning. She took the bottle wordlessly blushing and passed it under the red beam of the barcode reader.

'And you,' she managed, trying to smile back through the maelstrom of disorientation that was ricocheting in her.

'I've never been in here before, I'm just going to dinner with a friend nearby,' he said indicating the bottle as if that explained everything whilst she grappled with who the friend might be, 'but it's great to discover you here.' His voice was delicious.

'Yes, just open the door and here I am,' she ducked behind the euromillions scratch card stand then popped out waving in one flourishing movement.

'Well now I know where to find you I'll call again,' he said bowing graciously.

She curtsied and said 'please do.'

And he was gone. Sheer delight coursed through her as she scanned the twin baby lettuces and unripe tomatoes for the next customer.

☐

The next morning was a rare bright day when winter relents from its grey insistence and dawns in crystal clarity, when cold is welcome because it comes from clarity, cutting through drudge and electrifying senses sideways with its low slanting light. Karen and Matt were eating breakfast together.

'Brutal weather' he said, 'what an amazing view. I don't think I've seen it so clear before.'

'Have you been running again?'

'Yep, I woke up early even though I was totally knackered last night. I wanted to get a good start, I'm going to move the car and ask Joe about the gate, I've done a bit of a diagram for what needs doing he said he'd help,' he took a slurp of hot tea listening to the enthusiasm in his voice. 'I can't believe this is happening really, it's like I stepped into a dream.'

'Glad you think so.' She sipped hers thoughtfully. 'It's good for me too and Joe probably.'

'He's the man, isn't he? Totally crazy guy. How long have you known him?'

'Well, I wouldn't say I know him exactly but ever since I moved here he's helped me out with stuff. He's been a great neighbour, he's a fair bit older than me.'

'But man, he's fit, he worked alongside me all day. I reckon he's had quite a life.'

'Why, what did he tell you?' She was curious.

'Just stuff,' said Matt not sure how much to report, 'maybe we could get him round one time.'

'Sure, let's' she said. 'Listen, I've got to go, I've got a job on this morning. I'll see you later.'

'Where's your car parked then?'

'The neighbour the other side lets me use her drive, in return for putting the bins out, otherwise there's nowhere to leave them, these places predate the motor vehicle by a long chalk where to leave your car is a bit of an issue, commoners owning cars has only just been allowed!' She made a grovelling face and laughed. 'I'll see you later, have a good day.'

Matt rinsed the breakfast things and followed her out the door. He crossed the frosted ground flipping his car keys back and forth in a hand jingle. Life, it could be good. The valley shone, hills lapping and overlapping in the middle and far distance, wooded outlines detailing field edges and at the far horizon an undulating body of hills danced with the sky. Beauty, the world was full of extraordinary natural beauty.

The indicators flashed amber as the car doors clicked open. The synthetic air freshener swinging from the rear-view mirror assaulted his nostrils. Fresh air really did improve your sense of smell, the chemical perfume hit his nose like a mallet, so he ripped it down and almost threw it out of the window before reminding himself where he was. Pulling into Joe's yard moments later he parked up close to the hedge where the car couldn't be seen from the road. Clutching the diagram of the gate he dropped the noxious air freshener into Joe's wheelie bin then went straight round the back of the cottage to his workshop.

Sean couldn't sleep watching shadows and lamp post lights filtering through curtain cloth to play patterns on the ceiling. They sent shards through his eyelids, along the neuropathways

to create a maze of confusion in his beleaguered brain where he was already lost. Only morning brought the relief of natural light, and he finally found the darkness of unconscious slumber. It was past noon when he awoke and after the excruciating effort of actions once fluidly automatic, a triumphant arrival into the bathroom after the exertion of walking, the slow expulsion of urine and shit, sphincters needing to contract, turning a tap to shower water onto the body, then having to towel away the water, putting on clothes, it was all such a slog. Eating and drinking: another mass of many details of energetic requirement, the weight of the kettle, the turn of another tap, the heavy resistance in the fridge's door, the reach towards the toaster. By 2pm he was exhausted but finally ready. Only a couple of hours before the daylight wore out. At least the driving was some sort of comfort, for a press on a pedal resulted in considerable reward and he was seated. The motorway was quiet, so he drove fast and felt disproportionately powerful, arriving at the warren of leafy lanes sooner than he had anticipated.

The little carpark was empty save for an idling supermarket delivery truck, thankfully not one of his firm's. The driver was shut eyed leaning back in his seat catching zeds in a quiet moment. Sean took a mental snapshot of his former rivals before realising that he didn't really care anymore but the driver as if cognisant of criticism came to and drove off.

There was no blue car to be seen. He texted Ray, a moment later receiving a terse reply. *find the house then. See if they know anything.*

Beyond the 'access only' gate a grand hill sat like a giant at dinner dominating the foreground where snack like sheep were pastured. There was a stone track with a slow incline rising to a hedge line on the right. Sean set off thinking to find a high point from which to look about. He hadn't gone more than a hundred

143

metres when tucked away below he saw a gathering of trees where amongst the branches the giant's cigarette was giving off smoke from an ashtray chimneypot. Interrupting the hedge was a collapsing wooden gate. The fairy tale spell lured him towards it and as if somnambulant he found himself in a cultivated yet untamed garden. A garden path wound through smaller leafless trees and opened onto a long-haired lawn with flowerbeds sleeping on all sides. A couple of stone steps took you to the door of a stone cottage. He hesitated, wondering how to explain his presence when the front door opened suddenly. He heard the voice before he saw her.

'I thought I heard someone…..' her voice faltered on seeing him and stammered to silence as he stood stunned before the figure of the woman who had used the faulty pump on his supermarket's forecourt, when was it? Another lifetime ago.

'What are you doing here?' The woman commanded, fierce, unfriendly.

'I, er I'm looking for someone?'

'In my garden? Trespassing on my property?' Her eyes glittered with armoured defiance, 'who exactly might you be looking for?'

'His name is Matt, we saw his car.'

'And who is we?'

'Me and his boss, he's worried about him.'

'Never heard of him, now get out of my garden or I'll call the police.'

Sean turned to go, wanting to be as far away as possible from this woman who he somehow associated with his downfall but as if choreographed by the fairies in this dreamscape garden he halted and mumbled.

'I'm sorry,' then started to blub, a shocking wobbling boyhood chin quivering blubbery remorse. 'I'm sorry I made it your fault, it wasn't I know, please forgive me, please make it better.' He lowered his head in shame as if waiting for an axe to fall then shuffled backwards away from her immediate sphere of influence.

'Get out of my garden,' she roared, 'how dare you come here.'

He found himself back on the common expelled, trying to run, dragging himself back along the track to his car. The gloaming was gathering as the figure of a young man passed him having vaulted the gate with a nimble bounce, jogging back along the track and down towards the cottage. Was that him? He was dressed in a city style that was familiar.

Sean took out his phone and texted *No sign of him here* before he really knew what he was doing.

'What the fuck!' Shrieked Karen as Matt stepped jauntily through the front door. He'd spent another day with Joe, learning how to sharpen tools and all the various ways you could fix a gate. Ranging through chainsaw techniques and planes, to chisels and clamps, the two men had synchronised interest and expertise, inspecting the difference and tolerances of wood and the trees they were the bodies of. Matt had listened to Joe's tales entranced, told in the manner of a great adventurer and now his head was saturated in the deliciously satisfying way that a perfect doughnut holds oil and jam, just waiting to ooze out into the bite. Matt couldn't wait to get stuck in.

'Did you transfer money to me? Is that how they tracked you here? I'm surprised they didn't nab you on your way back from Joe's, it's a miracle you didn't bump into that bloke and end up in the boot of his car.' She was shaking, pacing around the small kitchen with furious turns and fidgets, shoulders held in anxiety almost bumping her ears.

'Woah hold up a minute. What are you talking about?' Instinctively he put an arm around her shoulder, hoping to settle her. 'Who has been here?'

She shrugged, twisting way from the attempt at comfort, turning towards Matt and explained in a cool steel tone: 'Just now, this bloke asking about you, I told him to eff off, but fuck's sake he was here in the garden, looking for you and you know the weirdest part of it?' She didn't wait for a reply, 'I've met him before at a petrol station a month or so ago, the bastard tried to blame me for a broken fuel pump. Never in a million years did I think he'd turn up on my doorstep, what the hell is going on....'

'Karen, what did he look like?' Matt asked, now infected with worry.

'Bulky, burly, almost bald and well, kind of broken.'

That didn't fit the description of either Ray or Saunders, one was a weasel and the other a hairy specimen. 'Well, that's neither of the guys I worked with and no I haven't transferred any money, you said not to, so I didn't. It won't be that. There was a car up there just now as I passed by and yeah there was a bloke but no one I recognised. I thought he was some sad out of shape guy trying to go for a run. Maybe someone's seen my car before I took it to Joe's.' An image of Matt's encounter with the woman from kung fu slipped into his mind. 'Hang on though, the day I arrived, there was a woman I know vaguely, I bumped into her in the car park, but she wasn't anything to do with work,' his voice trailed off.

'What! you met someone you know up here? And didn't think to tell me?'

'I didn't think it was relevant, I was in a state, I'd just got out of the city.'

'Not relevant? Matt are you thick or something, it's a huge elephant coincidence.' She sounded exasperated. The steel becoming sarcasm, Karen was now looking at him as if deciding whether to keep it bottled or fully lose it. Enough had already leaked out, corrosive. It had been a massive mistake to come here, why had he ever thought it could possibly work out, he needed to move on, there was nothing to salvage from the blame.

'Listen,' he said with more assurance than he felt. 'I never wanted to make trouble for you, you've helped enough but it was a stupid idea to think I could hide out here. I'll get going.'

She didn't argue.

'And I'm really sorry, I'm not a bad guy but I can't expect you to keep trusting me, it was some make believe kid thing. I was fooling myself.'

'Maybe I was too' said Karen bitterly. Although the fury had drained, storm water rushing downhill searching for a level, she was scoured out. 'What I can't get over is that I recognised the guy, he was so unpleasant I kind of cursed him.'

Matt responded wearily. 'There's a lot of nasty people involved but I don't know why one would be working at a petrol station, it's not like they'd need the money.'

'Maybe he just ended up there or was working as a front perhaps? But he was the supermarket manager, they brought him across because of what happened when the pump overflowed. You wouldn't think he'd have time to be a drug lord and run a big store.'

Matt had already stopped listening. He was disengaging from the chat, the warm fire, the companionship, the developing sense of home, the feeling of belonging. Upstairs he shoved his stuff back into the bin bags, ignoring the tentative beginnings of established relaxation, quickly scanning to make sure he hadn't left anything. For the briefest of moments, he wondered if this was all melodrama but snapped back to Karen and the men involved and regained the urgency to move. The bin bags grazed against his thighs, contents rustling and clunking impatiently as he made his way back to his car, struggling to work out what to do next. He had left the cottage hurriedly while Karen was out the back fetching wood. Once upon a time he had bungee jumped and the snap back at the bottom of the fall was just how it felt now. It was almost dark, the evening sky a regal velvet blue with a line of butterfly turquoise edging the day's brilliance before it plunged into obscurity. Quietly, not wanting to alert Joe to his departure he bundled the bags into the boot then slid into the driver's seat through the narrow gap allowed by the hedge. He wasn't exactly numb but had hardened like clay in air holding its shape, brittle and vulnerable to collapse, this was his to sort out. These people here had nothing to do with it. He left the headlights off, started the engine and drove onto the lane flicking on the lights once he was away from the property. If Joe had heard anything he didn't come to investigate.

There would be ice forming on the lanes, the flow of water halted by distance from heat, the sun on holiday at the other side of the world. Despite feeling estranged as Matt drove away he found that at the centre of his fear he was strangely, impassively present. Along a previously unchartered lane he pulled onto a track into a wood until a padlocked gate prevented further access, then turned off the engine. Grabbing his duvet from one of the bags he wrapped himself up on the back seat, considering his options until an unlikely sleep overtook him.

Chapter sixteen

It was early afternoon when Gus went back to the shop looking for Belle, although he still didn't know that was her name.

'She's not in today' explained the tired looking older man who was augmenting his pension with a couple of casual shifts.

'Could you give her this note for me please?' He had written it earlier just in case. Hello, it read, I run a martial arts class, if you wanted to come along, I'd love to see you, Gus. He left the class details and his phone number, it had taken him a long while to figure out how to write something safe and neutral. Nobody liked being stalked.

'Thanks,' he said to the man who placed the envelope beside the till. 'I'll let her know' he said, adding protectively, 'her name's Belle, she's a very nice young woman.'

Gus grinned and said Yes, I thought that too,' and for a moment the tiredness lifted from the older man's face.

☐

Karen sat resisting another glass. The house reverberated emptily licking its wounds, settling after the hurtful exchanges. She regretted shouting at Matt. If she hadn't, he might still be here. Hadn't she said they would work it out together when she had first offered for him to come here. Now fickle and weak willed, her trust had buckled at the first hurdle. The shock of sanctuary violated by that horrible guy appearing at her door, had punctured the self-protective bubble, blown recently to bursting point by the nature of Matt's arrival. She didn't need that kind of encounter on her doorstep. She thought about the man, confused as to how he had arrived here as if from another planet. He had seemed on the point of collapse mumbling apologies, as if seeking redemption. The convergence of events hadn't made any sense. She tried to reason the scenario into sequential sense, but it refused to adapt, the dimensions too obscure, the mystery of it was disorientating. It was almost as if he had been looking for her, as if Matt was purely incidental. He was dangling from the line she had cast, in cursing his violence. Somehow it had transpired that he was reeled in to ask for forgiveness and release. To grovel. Judging by the altered state of him whatever had been evoked had caused serious effect.

But it wasn't magical was it? Matt's presence had simply connected her to this underworld network of drugs and thugs. And that day he had treated her with utter contempt, so why should she be sorry, he had it coming, he was obviously an asshole. There was the entirely logical explanation. Reasoning thus, instead of cool relief logic's inadequacy brought further agitation. She became aware of a pivotal choice. Here was the turning, the unwinding of past wrongs.

Phosphorus, potassium, and glass powder combined with friction to combust. The matchstick head struck against the box, she lit a candle. The glow satisfied her. Why not kind magic? It was far more appealing than threat. No blame could ricochet into the future, no legacy drag responsibility screaming and kicking in consequence. Concentrating her mind on the lumbering man who had stood terrified and uncertain before her door, she recalled the moment of near pity she had fleetingly felt when the force of wrathful power had passed through her. It had been quietly nestling in the intensity of her rage, the vision of a boy turned mean. She had overridden compassionate instinct and instead hurled the full force of her derision at his nasty behaviour, to hell with him. Now forgiveness poured gracefully into her. Balancing on a knife edge she conjured a readjustment of the original encounter and recalled the curse. It would be too easy to cut herself on a sense of justification. Of victimhood. She unhooked the barb, threw him back to swim away. Years of painful recrimination lay stirring beneath these thoughts, of other travesties, a supermarket trolley of them, dumped in a water course collecting all manner of detritus in its metal caging. There would be more work to pick out the accumulation because the water was bringing flotsam and jetsam in its wake but for now she felt the gentle relief of pardon and knew that somehow it would reach his pathetic plea.

☐

Belle was on a short afternoon shift covering for a colleague who had a hospital appointment. It was by chance she saw the envelope tucked behind a stack of out-of-date special offer vouchers. She sighed, being the only one of the many staff who kept things organised she was just about to tidy it all into the bin when she noticed her name scrawled over it. Oh no, someone else wanting a favour, for her to cover their shift. She tucked it into her jeans back pocket as a stack of fruit corner yoghurts was placed precariously in a tall tower on the counter waiting to make it through the till. She'd only just finished cleaning up from a splattered coleslaw packet that someone had dropped and not bothered owning up. Stuff was often carelessly spilt, packets eaten empty while people went round the shelves, cartons drunk and left in the baskets. It wasn't her job to police the shop but sometimes it felt like people were taking advantage and she didn't like being taken for a mug. If too much went missing the managers suspected them, threatened to dock their wages. Today the drudge of it had got to her: sniggering teenagers, vomiting children, screaming parents, and doddering pensioners kept walking through the door with their stuff. Another day she could deflect a snidey quip from a fourteen-year-old with a laugh and a smile, a threatening mum needed a bit of sympathy, a tantruming child the space to scream and an older person an opportunity to chat. It was a relief to hand over at the end of the afternoon and she left walking briskly as the shadows yawned preparing for the night. She stripped off the working clothes and bunged them into the washing machine, on reflection checking the pockets for those demon tissues that floured and stuck to everything. Ah there was the note. Dreading another request on her goodwill she opened it reluctantly.

☐

It was predawn when the merciful sleep evaporated. He woke cold and cramped in the back seat of the car. Needing to pee he got out shivering and crunching on frosted twigs and deadened leaves then jumped up and down to get the circulation moving through his limbs. Instinctively after the days with Joe he looked at the wood lying around and started to gather bits and pieces, gleaning he had said it was called, an old commoner's right. Hunting through his belongings now scattered all over the boot he found a lighter, realising it was days since he had had a smoke. A few old till receipts and the twist of the lighter's wheel kindled a small flame in a clearing a short but private distance away from the car, and he gently fed the fire first with tiny twigs then with bigger sticks until he had a blaze. The cheer was immense. Fetching some larger boughs, he banked up the fire as it started to give out significant warmth and then he sat by it swaddled in the duvet. He watched the dance of the flickering flames bloom upwards and cascade, shapes moulded by the invisible hands of the wind. Consuming the wood hungrily the wind created caves in the fire where blue halos formed and disappeared amongst the reds whilst dawn rose as a light being awakening. This was how humans had always done it. Simple and free, the combustion of a tree was home and hearth. He felt safe, sure and at peace. A plan was forming. When eventually grey ash overtook the orange glow and smouldered with the last dregs of smoke, he reckoned it was safe to leave, packed up and headed back towards the city, hunger driving.

☐

For the first time since his 'fatigue' had begun Sean woke refreshed and with an appetite. Instead of joining the family at breakfast however, he kept to his room contemplating his next move. It wouldn't harm to keep a little separate for a while longer and as his sense of self seemed to be reintegrating into his body, he found plenty to reflect on in solitude. Ray had replied with some unpleasant put down but hadn't pursued the matter and then there was that extraordinary chance meeting with the woman and the coincidence of feeling cautiously better afterwards. The ducks were lining up he thought. He would take aim. Once he had heard all the family leave the house, he showered and dressed, venturing into the marital bedroom for a change of clothes. He wanted to throw away the clothes he had been wearing as if they cast a spell to be rid of and decided he would. In the wardrobe an embarrassingly long row of shirts stretched along the rail, he picked a pale pink one he had never worn before. Cathy had bought it for him, he had found the colour ill chosen, but now topping it with a pale grey jacket and the blue of his jeans gave him a good feeling when he looked in the mirror. He'd lost muscle tone but a few trips to the gym would soon sort that.

The final flourish was a dab of aftershave and an opening of the window in his musty den. After a quick call he left the house and headed for a newly furbished café for breakfast. It wasn't far from where he had made the appointment for later in the morning. Choosing a window seat he polished off a full English sensitively presented on a wooden platter then sat back over a second cappuccino to digest, look about and edit his story. He was glad to be in the hubbub of the place, it was popular, they were doing good trade: honest and hardworking, they deserved it. Unlike Ray's nasty, dishonest world.

Matt pushed open the door of the café. The smell of the food made him salivate. He hoped he didn't look too grungy and remembered the only other time he had been here, smart but nervous. He ordered a large breakfast, popped to the toilet to wash his hands and face, approving of the stubble shadow and beginnings of subtly wild transformation in the mirror, it was as good a disguise as any. He then tucked himself comfortably into a corner seat at the back of the place where he could watch the whole room.

If Sean had been noticing he might have recognised the familiar gait, a figure who had leapt a gate, a recently encountered outline. But as the food settled in his stomach and people came and went to the tinkle of the bell, he had begun to feel it was time to get on with it and, apprehensive, had ordered the bill, paid and left. However innocent you are the police will instil a certain feeling of wariness, as if you about to be rumbled, it's their job. Sean wasn't a stranger to police contact. They had a special instore liaison officer because people were always thieving from his store. He had often used the threat of them. Today, he cleared his throat and gave the desk sergeant the name of the detective he had made the appointment to see. He was shown into a non-descript interview room and looked about checking if there were any two-way mirrors or filming devices trained on him. His mouth was now dry and heart hammering when a middle-aged woman with a pleasantly bland face came into the room. 'So, how can I help? I was told you want to make a statement.' She sounded kind.

It was a slow afternoon for everyone. Despite the attempts to ramp up for yet another festive season there was a quietness that came in with the cold. The desire for hibernation resisting clocks' time wants to suspend the ticking and go still. Matt chose the library as the warmest place to be anonymous and struggled to keep his eyes open over the book on carpentry he had picked from the rows of shelves.

Please come back tonight Karen had texted *I'm sorry I overreacted. Snow forecast for the next couple of days and the lanes will be unpassable you'll be safe here.*

Thanks, he replied, leaving it open in his own mind because it all depended. He could let her know later. Having the offer was the thing though, it was a brace. There were people who cared. But he wasn't a child and he had to resolve this situation himself, the rejection made him wary even though deep down he knew he could trust Karen and Joe. He looked around the library at the crumpled assortment of individuals and felt the stirrings of sympathy with the unknown lives of others. He hadn't been in here since he was little when they would come in together, his mum helping to choose the big, illustrated books that seemed like elaborately coloured worlds between covers. The building had subsequently been modernised and somehow diminished in the refurbishment. Plastic superseded wood and strip lighting erased nuance. The electronic bank of computers encroached on the once still space of paper, ink and board, the solid dream of thoughts had been transformed into electromagnetic current.

Others in here sat at desks or on the padded seating areas working studiously or simply settled in the library as a surrogate home, a last bastion of social responsibility where people could rest and use the toilets and maybe sometimes a kind librarian might make them a sneaky cuppa. Matt thought of homelessness not as a lack of roof and walls but as a profound disenfranchisement from belonging anywhere. For those few days up on the hill he had thought himself at home. He longed for a life where he belonged. Perhaps he would go back there later. He would see what he could find out. Whoever it was who had visited will have reported what: that his car was no longer there, that the woman of the house had sent him packing? The possibilities seemed endlessly mutable. The heat was soporific, the cold night on the car's seat pulled down his heavy eyelids, and head bowed he napped, the book on his lap a disguise.

It was already dark when the library turned out the last remaining heat seekers. He figured he would drive to the hall and wait until the class started. Hopefully she'd turn up and then he could ask her. Christmas lights flickered feebly, wobbling on wires strung between buildings. Reindeers and snowmen, santas and holly swayed above the streets like feeble talismen, while lamp posts sported star tiaras. He drove on through the shopping area into undecorated backstage streets where the real community lived. The hall sat in darkness. He parked and waited.

Chapter seventeen

It was a chilly interlude until Gus came sauntering along with the air of a man who had won the lottery. Matt was warmed by the sight of him but slipped further down in his seat so that he couldn't be seen in return. It was all too much to explain. The doors unlocked, the lights switched on and the whole atmosphere of the place lifted as a warm glow filtered out. Light in the darkness, the city's electric answer to his morning's fire. Some others straggled in; their thick winter coats bundled up. Then in rode the dark-haired woman dismounting on the move, stopping at a parking sign pole where she started to padlock her bike. Matt was out of the car, the flash of indicators obeying the electronic command, Lock! and striding over before she had a chance to register his approach.

'Hi,' he was nervous now as she looked up startled by the sudden appearance of someone appearing from the dark. 'Sorry,' he garbled stepping back in placating retreat 'but would you mind if I ask you something?'

Alice was wary. What was it with this guy always showing up when she least expected him and now looking strangely altered. His sharply barbered hair had grown out enough to lose the neo military style and it was difficult to describe, but he looked as if he had loosened up somewhere, uncertain but freer. The effect was unnerving.

'Well, class is about to start, but what is it? I was worried about you the other day. Wondered if you were in some sort of trouble.' She heard herself sounding professionally condescending which belied the more honest irritation she felt in his presence.

'Basically, er I've been on the run' he said, 'not because I've hurt anyone but I'm trying to get away from someone who might want to hurt me. And I have been wondering if you know them.'

There was a moment's potent silence.

'What?' Alice shrieked, her irritation now unstoppable, 'I beg your pardon. Who the hell do you think I am? What are you implying?'

'It's just only you knew I was up there and then someone came looking for me and Gus texted and so I wondered. I'm trying to work out how they found out where I was.' Matt faltered as he watched her face crumple in disbelief then resolve into intense dislike.

'You worked out I must have dobbed you into your criminal fraternity. Is that it? That is unbelievable.' She flapped her arms like a fledgling attempting take off. 'And then I told Gus, and you think Gus is some sort of a double agent for the mafia? Christ you are paranoid. You sad fuck.'

Matt felt a flood of shame as she stomped into the hall, leaving him standing outside ridiculous and belittled. What was worse, he would have loved to go in and be that fluid creature who had prospered under the benign gaze of a teacher. The exclusion was excruciating, but no way could he walk in there now with her frothing at the mouth. It wasn't at all how he'd imagined the conversation would go but what had he expected? She was over the top reactive. What did she have against him? The build-up of pressure peaked, he turned back towards the car. From the other direction Belle approached the hall hurrying nervously, in the end she had delayed arriving at class early, not wanting to appear too eager. In her excitement she failed to recognise the back of the man unlocking the blue car as she pushed open the old gym's door.

Some may call them angels or fairies, benevolent ancestors, or the spirits of place but tonight Matt felt a blessing that was gently anaesthetic, that soothed the onslaught of Alice's anger and opened a channel that discharged her fury and his shock. He texted Karen to say he would return to the common, he had at least got a clear answer that Alice wasn't anything to do with a betrayal. He could let Karen know and calm the nagging doubt that someone else might go up there looking for him. If they did, he wanted to be there.

Inside the hall Alice was furiously trying to calm herself down from a near apoplectic rage. The guy was not only an insane narcissist but an extraordinarily appalling judge of character. As if she would be involved with an illegal racket, somehow knowing to follow him up there to the hill to inform the gangster boss, what a fantasist. But as the warmup breathing exercises switched on her parasympathetic nervous system, she began reluctantly to see why it wasn't as absurdly outrageous as it first appeared. She knew enough about illicit dealings and where they could end. A lot of the kids she dealt with had suffered as a result, with family members falling foul of the law or other hierarchies that left the children alone, defenceless, and possible prey. He wasn't to know she was herself strung out from trauma overload. The class continued providing opportunity to vent both coagulated frustration and buried sorrow until it even started to seem quite plausible that she could be cast in the role of informant. She allowed herself the daydream of a criminal alter ego, villainously operating on a parallel plane as she practised kicks and blocks in a partner exercise. Her partner was an older man, heavy set and unresponsive and for a fleeting moment she imagined Matt flying through the moves with enviable grace. It was becoming an effort not to regret her accusatory outburst as she finished practising with the lumpen adversary.

At least there was another younger woman in the group tonight. She gave off a slightly glamorous air, a fair and peachy shimmer rippled around a gentle open face that smiled easily. A little younger than Alice or maybe simply less careworn, Gus seemed to be paying her a lot of attention, their laughter was unashamedly infectious. Alice stifled a tinge of jealousy as she saw a current of delight running between them. She felt the whirr and click of her connection to Gus move in readjustment.

After class they all went around the corner to the Dog and Bucket for a drink. Many small local pubs were having a hard time surviving the competition of cheap carry outs and home entertainment. The D and B was a community triumph having been bought by an inspired crowd funding initiative and then run as a cooperative. The Pub's sign was currently painted with a cheeky terrier in shades on the beach, a bucket and spade hanging off his perky tail. Last month it had been a seated deerhound with a cloth bucket held in its paw like a handbag. Another time a spaniel teetering on a ladder with wallpaper glue slopping from a bucket. Labiadoodle, the feminist artist collective, regularly repainted the sign, before which the soon to be whitewashed images were immortalised as photos and displayed on the walls of the pub, creating a growing gallery of canine portraits through the various eras of the establishment. It had acquired the reputation of a happening venue drawing a crowd from across the city. There were regular band nights, comedy slots and cabarets but tonight it was empty apart from the class members and a few regulars.

Belle, Gus and Alice sat at a table together.

Gus had excitedly introduced them and now close up Alice could almost smell their blossoming compatibility.

'I loved the class,' Belle was saying, beaming at Alice, her smile magnetic.

'How did you hear about it? Alice asked intrigued.

Belle shoved Gus playfully on the arm, 'he happened to come into the shop and told me that he taught a class.' Alice could see that Gus was totally smitten.

'Where do you work?'

'Oh, it's just local to me. It's terrible pay but the shifts are flexible and most of the time I enjoy the people.' Belle blushed suddenly self-conscious. 'What do you do?'

'Me, I'm a gangster,' Alice joked but sounded horribly sarcastic.

She saw Belle react, confused by the flippancy and unsure of the context behind the remark. Gus, disapproving, chipped in, 'so have you had a radical change of career this week?'

'No. Look I'm sorry. I work in child protection, but just before the class this bloke Matt jumped out of the darkness and he kind of accosted me, accusing me of betraying him to the mob. I suppose I haven't fully recovered yet.' She smiled sheepishly.

'What? Matt was there at the gym? Why didn't he come in? I thought he was taking time out for a while, wouldn't be around.'

'Well, he just appeared as I was locking up my bike and said he was trying to dodge some people who didn't wish him well but then said he reckoned I might have something to do with it because of the other day up on the hill. Fucked up or what?'

Gus whistled. 'So, he is in trouble. Blimey. What did you tell him?'

Alice's face burnt. She stared down at the table willing the temperature of her skin to cool. 'I shouted at him' she admitted quietly. 'I was still pissed off after all that worrying the other day. I pretty much told him where to go. I've got enough high drama to deal with at work without his.'

Gus was watching her cautiously. 'So where did he go after that?'

'I don't know,' she almost whispered. Speaking it out she was shocked now by her harsh behaviour and felt a plummeting sadness. 'I suppose I didn't handle it very well, everything's all been too much lately I think I must be burning out. I'm sorry I didn't have any spare kindness in me.' Tears pricked at her eyes.

Belle gently placed a hand on Alice's arm. 'If it's the Matt I know too, neither did I. He's not straightforward, doesn't make it easy. But this underworld story makes sense.' The two women took it in turns to piece their insights into Matt's identity. 'I mean regardless of what he's been into, he wasn't nasty or anything, just lost and well, alone,' concluded Belle.

And the three of them sat together bonding over the details of how people could fall into trouble of any kind. So Matt was caught up with a bunch of violent men. What a weary male stereotype. Gus shook his head. Whenever he worked the clubs, he was reminded of the testosterone posturing and bravado that, fuelled by alcohol and drugs, could kick start adrenaline, and inevitably lead to violence. It escalated in a moment and then blood spattered, and teeth flew, bones crunched and flesh tore. It was an ugly mini war expressing hostility and seeking power, an outlet in a system designed to disempower. A large part of the attraction of martial arts had been as creative self-defence on angry streets, a counterbalance to mindless battering. He had discovered later the fascinating philosophy behind it and had wanted to share that, wanted the fight to end. Gus liked Matt instantly when he'd first walked into class, he had sensed a similar disposition. Now he actively wanted to help him. The challenge for men was to assert themselves in healthy brotherhood, to reclaim their honour from the massacre of battlefields and misogyny.

☐

Meanwhile Matt, totally unaware that he might ever be at the centre of anyone's conversation, was heading into a blizzard. He had stopped at a large out of town supermarket shopping with forecast panic: tomorrow would be a trek across impenetrable mountains, a lonely desert devoid of oasis, all shelves bare. Pragmatically he also wanted to take some treats for Karen and Joe and there was the need for comfort after rejection. He then filled up with petrol before driving on into the worsening weather. He used his debit card. Fuck 'em, that could cause confusion as to his whereabouts. Hi boys, I'm right under your noses, yoohoo! over here out in the hills.

The snow started falling slowly at first, as occasional pieces of white fluff billowing in the winter sky. Before long, huge snowy flakes, each crazily individual swirled around in the night's darkness defying the windscreen wipers to maintain a path of clear vision ahead. The main roads instantly transformed any whiteness to a gritty brown sludge churning under the wheels of vehicles desperately bound for home. But as the roads narrowed to lanes the white snow was settling, and by the time he arrived at the bottom of the steep bank leading up the hill, it was compacted like icing sugar with a few tyre tread indents as decoration. The hedgerows and trees were laden with the visitation, drooping under the burden of their cloaked boughs. He had to take the hill in first gear. Several times the car slid and slipped backwards but with gentle persuasion he managed to gain enough traction to crawl whining to the brow and along the straight where he finally turned into Joe's yard and cut the engine. That had been a ride way more exciting than any computer game he'd ever played, and the exhilaration of real success stripped out some more of his earlier stress.

This wild cold weather biting at face and fingers sent surface heat diving inwards. It ignited aliveness inside, there was survival to consider. Arriving back safely he entered a divine fortress and was flooded with a deep sense of gratitude. If it carried on snowing like this no one else could possibly follow him here. The great forces must be listening to send such protection. The gates to the citadel were closing behind him but he had reached safety. He retrieved his hat from the pile of clothes and bedding, pulled it down over his ears and wrapping himself in his jacket gathered up the rest of the strewn belongings back into the bin bags along with what shopping he could also handle. The rest could wait until morning, the car would be colder than a fridge anyway. Trudging once again back across the common to Karen's cottage he decided as he went that all the coming and going was clearly a way of indecision, a waste of effort and too much drama. Although the city was only just over an hour's drive away it was a completely different world, and he preferred the trees and sky, unfettered nature and the blanket of white silence on the hill. They were the new blank page on which he would describe a different future that wasn't simply a choice of hideout. Apprehension swelled however as he neared the cottage, an awkward sense of responsibility for his effect on others stung and prickled. Nonparticipation was no longer an option. Total disconnection doesn't function. The front door opened leaving a swathe of banked up snow standing in mid-air like a starched and swagged curtain and Karen appeared squealing delightedly and hugging him vigorously.

'You made it! Am I glad to see you, how were the roads, quick take off those trainers they're soaked, have you eaten, bloody hell Matt you had me worried. Looks like we're in for days of this. It'll definitely foil any assassination plots. Tell me what news? Ooh shopping!' She gradually wound down and looked at him steadily. 'I really am sorry Matt, I shouldn't have shouted at you about that guy. I was just so shocked.'

Matt interrupted her. 'No Karen, it's me who should say sorry for bringing trouble to your door.'

'Can we both forget about it then? The thing is that guy was more interested in asking me for forgiveness than finding you.' Thank God you decided to come

162

back. I'm very happy to see you. I was dreading being snowed in alone.' And she told him the story of the incident at the petrol station. By the time they had finished their separate accounts of the previous day it was time to rest and sleep. Matt was exhausted.

The visitation of snow is as of royalty. It is not an everyday occurrence and demands preparation if you don't wish to be caught short without a log pile, emergency candles, spare batteries, enough food, and a snow shovel. Barring hurricanes, floods, tornadoes, tsunamis, earthquakes, and years long drought, snow is one of the UK's weathers that commands considerable regal respect. Perhaps because it is white, slippery and has a history of hiding everything under its carpets. Or that its unique crystalline formations describe water in mind staggeringly multitudinous patterns. Once arrived, snow allows all and sundry the chance to skid downhill extremely fast to their hearts' delight and their limbs' jeopardy. Snow stops us in our tracks, quietens and muffles, it is a clean slate, an insulating force, heavens' frozen blessing, business as usual's curse. Burying details, its blanket unifies distinctions. Road traffic mayhem, rail tracks' icy disruption, power cuts and freezing pipes, commercial chaos; whilst Jack Frost and the snow queen reign in their ice crystal crowns, the plans of the plebians must wait for the thaw.

Chapter eighteen

All the concrete, tarmac, bricks and mortar, heating systems, electrical cabling, human proximity, cars and carpets, cookers and fridges contribute. The raising of the ambient temperature challenges the wild nature of a place. The weather's impact on Sean was minimal in his well-insulated house. That was the way he liked it: warm and invulnerable. His mind had sharpened considerably during the day, stropped against the details of the plan. His body was beginning to reintegrate. Having managed a session at the gym despite his fitness compromised by sluggish weeks, he was confident that he could firm up the flab without too much trouble. The return of mental acuity was a huge relief. Feeling valiant and incorruptible, he was waiting expectantly. All he needed was the phone to beep with an incoming text containing details and instructions. Entirely self-motivated, Sean was seeking revenge. He wasn't thinking of a wider justice, that the vast demand for the numbing effects of heroin, marijuana, and cocaine would continue despite governments' loud bemoaning of the effects of drug abuse on society. He wasn't interested in why there was such a market in the first place, that caused misery from start to finish. For the peasant farmers across the globe far from the comforts of economic privilege, who were forced to produce illicit crops that created a lucrative revenue for vicious drug cartels, Sean had not a thought. Nor for the degraded human misery of addiction at the other end of the supply chain. No, Sean was interested in the glory of redemption and the settling of a score, the wider implications of his self-righteousness didn't figure. He was impatient, wanting the phone to signal the start, the ref's whistle to get the ball rolling, his goal was Ray's downfall.

☐

Britain was in the grip of the fiercest winter spell in years. Meteorologists were regularly interviewed; weather reports gave traffic light warnings on the hazards. Tucked up snug in the little cottage however, Matt could finally relax. Mounds and troughs of snow sculptures balanced frozen towering above the original contours of land. Laundry blue reflections glanced in at the windows during the short hours of daylight. The snow clouds had cleared, their departure heralding a plummet in temperature and a deep freeze. Translucent icicle teeth clung from the eaves, feathering ice crystals bloomed inside the window glass and refracted colours sparkled, shimmering like rainbow gems strewn across the ground.

Squeaking and crunching his way through knee deep snow crust Matt squinted in the glare and the swaddled silence. He had found an oversized pair of ancient wellingtons in the tool shed, had borrowed a bulky woollen jumper and pair of long thick socks from Karen, and Joe had dug out a lumpenly padded wax jacket from underneath his work bench. He had no idea what he looked like and cared less. It was liberating. Years of trying to make just enough of an impression and not totally disappear, to fit in but not stand out, had been exhausting. The afternoon after he arrived back in the blizzard, he had paid Joe a visit.

'Ah here you are, 'Joe said as if he'd been expecting him. 'Rough on the roads last night, was it?' Matt described his quest for Joe, including the smallest detail to enliven the story for his friend.

'Sounds about right' he replied enigmatically, 'I thought you were in a spot of bother when you first came up here. Then when your car was suddenly gone, I knew something was up. But I didn't doubt you'd be back and I'm glad you are.' Any residual distance between the two men was swept away. Neither had the capacity for direct acknowledgement of their mutual regard but rapport, a silent handshake, was now firmly established. 'I hope this freeze doesn't go on too long,' Joe confided, 'it's too treacherous to try and get off the hill.'

'Why would you want to?' Asked Matt innocently. 'It's perfect for me! Have you got enough food in? I bought plenty back, it's in the car, it's like a fridge in there.'

Joe grinned then gazed at his hands. 'Plenty of grub here thanks but my wife, she still gets distressed if I don't show up every other day or so.'

Matt didn't know what to say. He had thought of Joe as an independent loner who perhaps might have been a bit roguishly popular with women. Not as a married man with a wife.

'You're married?' He asked clumsily. 'Where does your wife live?'

'Yes, I am. Jen went into a care home just before Karen moved here, it was good to have a friend who didn't know any history, like a fresh start so I've never had cause to mention it. Besides I wouldn't want anyone's pity. It's a cruel illness losing your grasp on things, I didn't want to publicise it to preserve Jen's dignity. She was a very smart woman. I just couldn't look after her properly.'

'That's harsh Joe. I'm so sorry. You must miss her.'

Joe shook his head, in confusion more than denial. 'I miss the woman I used to know but as she got sicker truth is it was a strain to know what to do for her, wandering around lost and fretful. I sometimes wondered if her life had any purpose and that was a horrible way to think. At least now I can try and give her the best of me when I visit. Even so she doesn't really recognise me but wants to have a visitor. Some days I can't understand where it all fits in life's plan, what's the point in taking away a person's mind but leaving them alive?'

'Maybe there isn't a point to it' Joe had fallen silent, and Matt knew better than to ask further. 'I don't know lad but what I do know is it's time for me to stop my chuntering and for you to get back out on the hill.'

That was when Joe had ferreted around under the bench and dug out the old jacket to hand to him, shaking it free from sawdust. 'You don't need those city slicker synthetic threads up here. Dress for the weather. It's the best fashion.' Joe's face and voice had drawn the curtains on the earlier confidence and returned to banter. 'Now get on your way before you break your neck on the ice in the dark.' And Matt had left him. The snow had suspended time and in the looming space it was clear. Everyone had a story. Lots of people were wound up and wounded. And suffering was a significant protagonist. You just had to let yourself be a bit vulnerable, so others could be too. The rest was all front and posturing and trying to keep up. As if it was a race. But what were they running from or towards?

A little unease lodged in Matt, he wondered if all the while he had somehow become too infatuated with his own pain, clothing himself in victimhood to the detriment of all else. He was sure that becoming a victim wasn't the point of pain but was he prepared to pick up a bag of responsibility when there were always plentiful hooks to hang blame from?

'What's up?' asked Karen with the intuition of a cat.

'Nothing really, just thinking about stuff. Would you tell me about your life Karen, why are you up here all alone, really?'

Karen hesitated then said 'Bank up the fire then, I'll make tea and I'll tell you as much as you want to hear, it's old history. I can see that being snowed in has got to you.' She smiled wistfully and filled the kettle.

☐

Down in town where the pavements were slippery with ice and the once pristine snow had become a slushy grey, Gus and Belle were indoors naked, twisted in bedding and each other, aware of nobody but themselves. They had left Alice unlocking her bike and had dived headlong into the mysterious mirror that is the intimate other. They became animals devoid of guile, compulsively fascinated by the chemical soup of mutual attraction. Never had the crook of an elbow, the rise of a pubic mound, or the nape of a neck hollowed in pleasure been so captivating. Immediate and total abandon was suddenly simple. They surrendered to each other and travelled towards the brink together, where they danced, then brimming over, arrived delighted. Again, and again learning their vocabulary until exhausted they dozed later to wake to their own warm smells, sticky fluids, and sweet kisses on shared breath, hearts pumping. They had found each other. It was a miracle. Both were due back at work the next day. Dreading the separation, they were already excited about reunion and the joy of rediscovery. They named it love.

☐

Finally, the iron fisted freeze started to relinquish its grip, and a text arrived lighting up Sean's phone. *Tomorrow 2.30pm* and the details of a new location, the address of a national trust car park somewhere northwest of the city. Despite his impatience, Sean now found himself teetering on the rim of a smouldering volcano, his treacherous plan undermined by an all hell will break loose trepidation that caused his heart to palpitate. On regaining his strength, he had begun to regret that impulsive visit to the police station. There were surely other ways he could have satisfied vengeance. He wondered if it wasn't too late to retract his statement and claim mental health distress. It seemed to be a card that bought you entry into all sorts of sympathies these days, he reckoned. Maybe the police had wondered about him anyway. However, a nagging doubt, its end caught like a loose thread unravelling, spooled through him. He had given the Police his name and contact details and those of his brother-in-law. In his vehemence he had been explicit about the assignments and where they were dropped off. Any cop following it up couldn't fail to unearth suspicious activity and he would prefer to be on that cop's side of the law, however vicious the backlash. The police had promised protection after all, they wouldn't have followed it up if they hadn't believed him. With his heart a woodpecker's beak in his ribcage, he picked up the phone and called to inform of developments, hoping that after all the sword of Damocles would fail to strike him when it fell.

☐

Alice phoned in sick. After all the angst driven moments before the decision to call it had been surprisingly easy. They had been unexpectedly kind at work and even suggested a few days' grace before she needed to contact a doctor for a fit note. Her camel's back had fractured with the barely hidden disdain on Gus's face when she admitted how she had reacted to Matt's dilemma. Without too much introspection it was clear that her feelings were disproportionate. When she had woken the next morning, she had known. Understanding even this much she could begin to admit the severity of the burn out smouldering unacknowledged, its smoke was suffocating her. She knew her tolerance must have scraped the bottom of its barrel to cause her to lash out at a near stranger.

Her parents lived in the flat lands of the east. It was to there that she fled from the city. Unexpectedly they had also been supportive in exactly the right way: Not asking too many questions, giving her the space she had always asked for. She could walk by the river, crunching with the dog as if snow was a biscuit, crumbling at each step dunked in the frosty path. By the second evening she was ready to admit to them that she was taking stress related sick leave from work. Alice had been dreading weary smothering sympathy, but her parents seemed pleased she was taking care of herself. Perhaps they were quietly blunting their own sharp edge of ambition.

About time too. Her mum didn't use those exact words but managed to say as much. She had been watching her daughter's vital life force pale and shrivel. Had refrained from comment, avoiding reaction. The dinner table was candlelit, a few grains of risotto rice glowed romantically lingering in the smears of a mushroom sauce, Alice's mum looked at her gently. 'I have often wondered why you chose such a challenging career. Especially when you had a natural love and flair for plants and flowers.'

Alice swallowed, unable to reply.

'It's taken me a long time to realise this,' continued her mother, 'but we only make anything better by loving what we do. I'm sorry I didn't fully understand that when you were growing up. I think I may have pushed you to succeed like I was trying to as a teacher. When your granny died, I don't think I knew how to make anything better for you or any of it. I couldn't understand how anyone could take the life of such a warm and loving woman. There wasn't any point to it.'

'It's ok Mum.' Alice waved her hand as if trying to dispel a swarm of grief.

'I think you may have taken on the job of trying to make sense of what was wrong.' She waded on regardless.

'Maybe,' Alice managed, 'but it's not your fault I thought I could save the world.'

'I don't exactly think it was my fault, but I would love to see you happy again.'

'Thanks Mum, so would I. I didn't know how much pain and misery is out there in the world. I can't bear it and I started to think that I should be sorting it all out. Finding that I can't is a bit of a relief.' They smiled at each other as the back door opened.

'I think we're in for a thaw,' said her father cheerfully as the dog shivered slush from his paws.

Since before she could remember Alice had held her mother at arm's length, their mutual pain at risk of mingling into overwhelm, but a short while later, on saying goodnight she found herself responding to the invitation to embrace. Tearfully the two women gently rocked back and forth, back and forth, until it seemed as if they were dancing to a mutual lullaby that would finally soothe the hurt and allow for rest.

☐

The policewoman from the crime squad to whom he had been assigned had repeatedly run through his instructions until Sean thought he was going to implode with the pressures of relentless detail. She was an unassuming woman who didn't look anything like the cops on TV, in fact lacked any notable characteristics at all. It was a blandness that made focus blur. She was so unrecognisable; she would have made a brilliant criminal. No one could have picked her out in an identity parade. Sean's mind was failing to concentrate on the numerous repetitions.

He was to proceed as planned to the destination, pick up the package and deliver it without any deviation from the expected routine. He would however be wearing a wire and tailed by a series of unmarked vehicles and was to do his utmost to stay in contact otherwise he might put himself at risk. Sean wasn't sure if this was a scare tactic to threaten him, after all they had no reason to trust him. He was stuffed if he didn't trust them so decided he may as well. Once safely away from the immediate areas of action he was to text Ray that he had completed the assignment and then go home where he would continue to be under surveillance. Meanwhile the police would wait until the drop off was retrieved and follow through with arrests once they had the chain of command clearly traced. They needed the entire gang for it to be a workable conviction. There was little purpose in simply taking in the couriers. Various people in the organisation had already been investigated before Sean had offered his services as an inside stooge. It was imperative that this be a clean scoop. Some of the men suspected of involvement had high up sources of protection. Timing must be precise to avoid a serious fuck up. Was that all clear?

Assuring them that it was he left the station at 1.15pm with the first car tailing him at an inconspicuous distance. The wire was under his shirt so that if he needed urgent assistance they would hear. It was less like a James Bond assignment and more a risk assessed preschool trip as he crawled along in the lunch time traffic to reach the motorway that was enroute to the destination. Now he was on his way the nerves of earlier had given way to the adrenalin push to get the thing done and over with. Once this business was all out of the way he could return to work and resume his life. With the regaining of his vitality the memory of his pitiful state was receding into a fragmented dream that he was beginning to doubt had ever existed. He switched on the radio and started to relax as the traffic picked up speed and the car cruised along to some easy listening. From the rear-view mirror, he could see the silver estate keeping pace and felt confident that all would be well. The timing was impeccable. Sean arrived at the car park a couple of minutes before 2.30pm. Mr Saunders had obviously seen him park up because seconds later he drew up in the space beside him. A medium sized cardboard box was handed over in broad daylight which he put in the boot of his car. Sean could almost feel the hidden whirr and click of cameras recording the moment, but nobody in sight batted an eyelid.

People were coming and going in their cars. For those arriving to look around the stately home, there was nothing of interest in a cardboard box. They wanted brocade and ancestral oil paintings, copper kitchen pans and tapestries, walled kitchen gardens and stories of ghosts in the library, a couriered box didn't deliver.

Mildly disappointed not to be able to visit the tearoom, Sean started the car again to drive straight back to the city industrial estate to drop off the box. The silver estate was still following and although the mission wasn't yet completed, any sense of danger or urgency was forgotten in the dull humdrum of the road. The sepia of a post snow world was a comedown after all the brilliance of anticipation.

Reaching the industrial estate, the indistinguishable road layout nearly foxed his flagging concentration, he hadn't bothered to reset the satnav. He drove straight past the turning for the plumbers' supplies, realising his error a couple of roads beyond. Turning around he watched a red hatchback reverse and reorientate itself nonchalantly, parking temporarily outside a motor parts warehouse.

Sean edgy now, retraced the way back through a maze of similarly constructed steel erected buildings. Relieved, he finally found the right turning, shadowed by the red car at a reasonable distance. Tension built again as he wondered whether the parcel would fit into the deposit box bolted into the corrugated wall but he soon found that with a bit of wiggling and persuasion, he managed to post it through and hear it drop to the floor of the interior. Job done he relaxed and drove the last few miles home with the radio on, leaving the cops to do their bit. The police had let him know they were already aware of the activities of this drugs racket; it meant a greater chance that Ray wouldn't realise his part in the betrayal. That was reassuring.

He didn't want out and out war because of the impact on his marriage and family life. Cathy was becoming less available and the more distant she became the closer Sean wished her to be. He had never thought of himself as dependent but as she withdrew, the less confident he was of his position. She had never seemed particularly fond of her brother, but family structures were unpredictable, despite his nasty tricks, loyalties of blood ran deep. Things had changed at home and for the first time he was painfully concerned about how he might fit into the rearrangement.

Chapter nineteen

Before the three of them were to dissipate back into the everyday slush of the thaw, Karen and Matt invited Joe over for food and to spend the evening together. Matt cooked from the ingredients of his extravagant pre blizzard shop, and they were now mopping up the left-over lasagne with some crusty garlic bread.

'That was bloody lovely, thanks lad.' Joe pushed back his chair as if to allow more space for his expanded stomach although he remained lean as a wolf.

'Yes, delicious' said Karen, burping ceremoniously. They left the table to sit in front of the fire.

'So, what are you going to do once the roads are clear if the gangsters come a-calling?'

'Don't bother beating around the bush' said Matt laughing at Joe's blunt honesty and discovering he had lost the prey's overwhelming sense of impending doom. 'I don't reckon they will. They've got bigger fish to fry. I'd never seen the guy that came up here, he didn't know me, he was probably one of Ray's lackeys. And Karen dealt with him, sent him away none the wiser.' He smiled knowingly at her.

'Agreed' said Karen, 'I'm pretty sure there's nothing to worry about on that score.'

She returned Matt's smile. 'Besides, there are still too many jobs to get on with here to waste time thinking of blokes somewhere else who already think too much of themselves.'

'Talking of work, Matty,' said Joe, 'I was wondering if you would be free a day or two a week to help with some wood deliveries.' Joe turned now to address Karen. 'I've got more work than I can handle, and what with the weather I could do with some help. I'll pay him. That's if you can spare him,'

'Hmm,' she replied, 'I suppose I could lease him out, what's it worth?'

'Hang on a minute, I'm my own man here.' Matt puffed himself up into a swagger. 'I've got my career prospects to consider.'

They laughed as the fire sputtered and a great wodge of snow slid from the roof to fallumph on the ground outside the window. Karen laughed. 'You can take up slush clearing for starters! How about a day's work a week for me in exchange for rent and then you can work for Joe as much as he or you want, with a review come the spring?'

'Sounds very good to me' said Matt and he feigned spitting on his hand as they did too and the three of them shook hands, shocked by how easy it can be to suddenly feel like you are in a team.

☐

It was the same evening and Sean was now fretfully waiting for news. Unable to control his impatience he occasionally checked outside. Yes, there was still a car parked across the road, slightly steamed up, displaying occupation by his surveillance officer. Cathy and the kids were not due back from a party until later and he was grateful once again they weren't here to witness his agitation. As the time ticked by however, he found he wanted them home to distract him from the many wild scenarios that were incessant through his nervous system. Something didn't feel quite right with this timing. When the phone eventually rang it jolted through him like a stun gun. The voice told him to come directly down to the station, he should ride in the surveillance vehicle. They were just outside.

'What news?' He asked the two officers who led him into an interview room.

In time-honoured double cop fashion one detective eyed him shrewdly, the other looking mildly amused. They started the recording equipment.

'On what evidence did you suspect that your brother-in-law was drug running?'

'We've been through that,' said Sean immediately on the defensive. 'I explained in my statement: Ray wouldn't explain what he was asking me to do, he blackmailed me basically, said it was on a strictly need to know basis, it was obvious it was dodgy. Why what's happened?'

'Plumbing equipment is what's happened. U bends, easy fit junctions, washers and PTFE tape. The box you delivered was full of plumbing supplies. This has been an incredible waste of police time. And a significant embarrassment.'

Sean took a moment. 'But you know yourselves there's a case to be answered, you said that you've been investigating this for months.'

'Indeed,' replied the unsmiling officer, 'but we were relying on you to deliver vital evidence, literally speaking. Now either you tipped them off or someone else did and whoever that was got their information somehow, with the result that we're now much further away from a conviction than we were the day you walked in here to unburden your concerns and they are now alerted to the fact that we were mounting an investigation.' This was explained in a weary monotone, sizzling with disdain, each syllable pronounced slowly. 'How do you explain it, the subversion of this operation? It's a fiasco and could be construed as interference and obstructing police business.'

'You're not seriously suggesting that you're turning this back onto me?' Sean was nearly shouting with frustration, 'I've risked everything: my life, my family, my livelihood, and reputation trying to do the right thing here.'

'Yes Sir, we do understand there have been some risks for you, but we have always had a question mark as to your motivation, and well, if you were to look at it from our perspective, it doesn't quite add up. We were willing, some may say foolish, to entertain your approach to us, give you the benefit of the doubt so to speak, but it appears our trust was misjudged. It is a very high-profile case and now seems to be a question of who was going to get thrown under the bus first. Unfortunately for you playing with the big boys has not only caused something of an accident but has put you in the frame. You seem to be the one that got squashed, there may be some plea bargaining that we would consider….'

and so it went on until Sean, tired of protesting his innocence finally fell silent after demanding to call a lawyer.

☐

Alice left her parents' place filled with reassurance. After a conversation over breakfast, she was reminded that to be a florist had always been her dream. People depended on flowers for all occasions even though they were never a necessity. And without them there is no beauty. Gracing a table, coffin, wedding bouquet, or birthday celebration, flowers uplift the event. They are the jewels of the plant kingdom, the fairies' crown, the decorative embellishment, the delight of the beholder. From tiny wild posies to the most extravagant designer arrangement, simple instincts respond to them.

The florist as human agent chooses and arranges, adds a collaborative aesthetic. What better occupation Alice couldn't imagine. The elation she felt when considering this didn't compare to the dull dread thudding in her chest cavity contemplating a return to the traumas of abandonment, abuse and neglect. It left her little room for doubt. But she had grown used to a comfortable salary, it was its own security. The capacity to manage rent and buy stuff without having to worry created a rut of dependency. Knowing that the burden of poverty featured significantly in the tragedy of her clients' lives, meant she would go cautiously, manage at least some changes, nothing needed to be dramatic, she couldn't handle that. But she wouldn't bottle out, there wasn't any amount that could compensate for earning in misery. She would research floristry training opportunities when she got home. Go part time to start with. Bolstered by a plan she had just quieted the inner conflict when a text buzzed in her phone.

Are you free in the next couple of days? From Gus. Relieved that he hadn't abandoned her in disgust she replied *Yes*.

Belle and I want to find Matt, can you come?

OK. She responded immediately before she had time to talk herself out of it. Not wanting to disappoint Gus further and happy to be meeting Belle again, it was also an opportunity to apologise to Matt. She still felt the insult of his insinuation but if she was making changes then a little humility wouldn't go amiss.

☐

The melt water left the lanes and fields slick, slippery, and mushy with mud, gullying down ditches and pooling in low puddles. Matt and Joe were busy hauling fallen timber to the yard for conversion into logs. They were kitted out for the job with boots and special trousers. Seasoned loads were waiting to go out for delivery to customers who had run low during the cold snap. It was dismaying how many trees and big branch limbs had been brought down by the weight of snow. Great bones of oak, beech and ash slowly stacked up as the men cleared tracks, lanes and bridleways blocked by the collapse of the trees' skeleton. Overwhelmed by frozen weight or levered free from sodden earth, like teeth released from eroded gums, the giants lay, felled. Matt felt sorrow at the demise of each mighty being splintered as easily as a matchstick. He marvelled at the ring growth, each as worthy of celebration as a child's birthday, holding the records of years' worth of weather and progress through time. Spicy odours were released from the wood as the chainsaw ripped through it, each species a different fragrance, density, and with distinct patterns on the bark. All around stood the next generation of young saplings waiting for their turn to mature, to delve deep underground and up to sky, earth and air mirrored in root and branch where insects and birds harboured, and the news of the woods was broadcast by the intelligent gossip of fungi swarming through leaf litter. It was clear that trees live in community and that when one fell there was both loss and possibility for others.

He would only ever be learning from these trees; he would never fully comprehend the complex life cycles; their longevity spanned many years beyond a human's. This captivated and humbled him. Joe was ageless as he went about his work. He was as at home in the woods as a badger in its sett and noticed animal tracks and nests that Matt would have overlooked had he not been shown. They worked together as comrades, collaborating on the variously demanding tasks instinctively, occasionally silenced to listen to the call of a bird. The stresses on a fallen bough were important to understand to prevent a kickback from either the ripping chain of the saw or the tree itself suddenly released from tension. The wrong cut could kill. They had to trust each other. Joe made sure to tell a couple of cautionary tales about what could happen if you didn't concentrate. It gave the work an edge as keen as any blade. Sharpening was important. Any person worth their salt needed to know how to sharpen tools said Joe. Stones, files, diamond pads, and strops ensured that the wood was sliced as painlessly as possible, an amputation caused the minimal disturbance to the rest of the tree. Amazed by how lucky he was to have such experience so generously imparted Matt was both grateful and baffled to have existed so long without this precious introduction.

By the end of the day, they had piled up enough wood to deliver all the orders and more. Weary but satisfied Matt loped across the common looking forward to a shower and food. Karen was out visiting a friend and so he lit the fire, washed and ate, looking forward to lounging about enjoying some solitude. It didn't take long however before he became fidgety. Having grown accustomed to the easy chat or comfortable silences of company, an empty feeling now overtook him. The quiet in the cottage reminded him of his first night here and the shady characters talking in the night. He went upstairs to retrieve his phone realising it had been days since he had turned it on. There was a string of messages from Gus, starting from that fateful night when he'd cornered Alice before the class, all asking if he was ok. The most recent was from earlier that day with a question about where he was and if they could meet. It sounded so concerned that Matt replied immediately. He told Gus he would be free the day after tomorrow, Joe was visiting his wife in town.

Great came the reply straight back. *I'll be with a couple of friends.*

Matt felt a twinge at the idea of a group visit, he wondered who they might be but then, remembering the fellowship of trees, allowed the innate trust he felt in Gus to soften its resistant grip. When Karen returned and Matt mentioned that a couple of mates from town were thinking of coming by, she was thrilled.

'I'll look forward to meeting your friends' she had said so enthusiastically that he momentarily felt awkward, stifled like a kid dropped off at secondary school by an unfashionable parent. Immediately regretful, he tried to cover up his reaction but already there was a distinct recoil as she added, 'well that is, if you want to introduce me.' Then left to sit in the living room.

If only relationships were simple thought Matt. After the night when she had told him her story, he was aware that deep down there was a huge vulnerability in her fierce independence that needed gentle treatment. But he had no real reference map for a woman's needs. Let alone a woman old enough to be his mum. She was supposed to be the one who knew stuff, the mother who took care of it. He had missed out on the evolution of the trust that a good enough parent can offer their child. In so many ways Karen fulfilled that role, so it was confusing when it seemed that he needed to supply something in return. He hadn't been shown the great give and take. He wasn't sure how he felt about being beholden to another. Sometimes it just seemed too complicated, and he wanted to run but already knew where running would get him so, taking a deep breath, he walked into the room after her.

'Hey Karen, I'm sorry. I just felt like a big kid then. A bit lost you know. These people, I'm not sure if they exactly are friends, I only know one of them and not even that well and I guess I'm a bit nervous.'

'Don't worry about it,' Karen replied, 'I was way too eager, desperate even. It touches something very painful for me that I missed out on getting to know my son's friends. Stupid really, I may not have liked them anyway.'

'Please let's meet them together, it'll be good to have you there.' How quickly a stab of pain can turn on a pinhead with a willingness to kind honesty. With that communicated they played a game of backgammon, Karen thrashing Matt with healthy gusto.

☐

When Alice received the text saying that Gus and Belle would pick her up in the morning, she regretted saying she would go. It was hard enough to describe this episode to herself, let alone anyone else. Burn out? Break down? Crisis? PTSD?

Whatever its name, having allowed herself to stop pushing through, it she knew she was now less defended. She wasn't sure it was wise spending a car journey with a newly loved up couple heading to visit a bloke who had managed to upset her on all of the few occasions they had met, in a location that had formerly been her private peaceful place. It would probably be much better to give it a miss. Reaching for her phone to excuse herself from the ordeal, a gap in the air opened and she heard a wordless reprimand. *coward, what are you afraid of?* Although millions of nerve endings inhabit the cerebral cortex, this wasn't a logical brain thing, it was a challenge coming straight from her heart. Putting down the phone, she drank a glass of water, figuring sensibly that perhaps she was dehydrated. Looking in the mirror she saw dark hair and eyes, an unsmiling mouth, and a body both slender and well-toned. Appraising this reflection as if it were not her own, she thought it lacked something quintessential. The stranger in the silvered glass though perfectly well enough formed, didn't look like she felt on the inside. Did that make her a lie? On a whim she rushed to the wardrobe and pulled out a favourite but rarely worn garment. It was a mid-length dove grey cashmere coat that had been her grandmother's. The label's style dated it to the 1970's although it was a timeless piece of tailoring. The chocolate-coloured lining was faded with streaks of sun blanched age but otherwise the coat was in mint condition. Sliding her arms into the sleeves and shrugging her shoulders into it she felt folds of protection and warmth encircle her. Perfect. This could be her armour. Looking once again she smiled and swung her body side to side twisting to view left and right like a model posing for a photographer. Again, a quiet pause and a very vague memory. Quietly and gently, allowing herself to be guided by these intangible messages she applied a touch of makeup. 'Sometimes we need a little war paint,' her granny had said. Now when she looked back at her reflection, she wasn't afraid to see the beauty that stared back at her.

Chapter twenty

The car journey turned out to be fun. Belle was excited to see Alice and they chatted like old friends. Gus, who had borrowed the car specially for the outing was enjoying the drive and playing chauffeur to the ladies. He explained that Matt and Karen were expecting them and had sent directions as it was not an easy place to find. The mention of Karen momentarily confused both Belle and Alice who then started to speculate as to who she was and how Matt had gone from being on the run to getting shacked up with a lady friend all in the space of a couple of weeks. Alice felt another tinge of irritation as if everything about Matt was designed to cause trouble, but she snuggled further into her coat and watched the passing hedges as they bristled by. On the final climb of the steep bank to the little carpark Alice took charge saying they may as well leave the car there as she knew there was no other place to park, they could continue on foot to the common following a satnav to find the exact location. Alice had not realised that down from the path that she usually followed a stand of trees masked a long hedge behind which a garden grew. The gate was newly fixed, a piece of fresh wood spliced into an older structure covered in orange lichen. The three of them laughed as they entered the enchanted garden. 'He's lucked out here' said Gus with a whistle as they wandered through a small area of fruit trees. He paused to take Belle's hand and kiss her as they passed an old apple tree. 'We'll have to invite ourselves back here in the spring when the blossom is out,' he murmured, and Belle smiled, flushing pink with delight.

Alice lingered behind feeling gooseberry awkward but also in awe of the place. Behind the far hedge was a view over valleys and hills that undulated like a healthy heart chart, hers lurched in quiet yearning. She would love to live somewhere like this. They were crossing the lawn when the front door opened and a tall woman around her mum's age stepped forward smiling bravely as if braced against a wind. She welcomed them, warmly shaking hands and inviting them into a low-ceilinged room where a log burner was counteracting the damp chill of the outdoors.

'Matt won't be long,' despite her friendliness she seemed nervous, 'he had to go down to the shops to stock up a bit, we've been snowed in here we didn't know exactly when you would arrive. Can I get you a cuppa?'

Belle watched her curiously as she left for the kitchen. 'She looks familiar to me,' she said, screwing her eyes as if to force an image recall. 'Probably came into the shop one time?' Gus suggested, but Belle with a slight shake of the head let it go. By the time the kettle had boiled Matt was coming through the front door with a couple of supermarket bags. 'Oh! you're here already' he stuttered, the sight of Belle and Alice shocking him silent. The ease and banter ceased abruptly. Feeling horribly shy he blushed, ducking into the kitchen to put down the shopping. Gus came in after him and without any ceremony wrapped him in a bear hug.

'Wow Matt! Am I relieved to see you; we have been properly worried about you hearing all kinds of scary stories about thugs on your tail but as it turns out here you are all cooched up with a fairy godmother. This place is amazing. What's been happening? How are you?'

Matt couldn't reply immediately, gagged by the uncomfortable configuration of people together in one place. Cautiously words not yet verbalised, words that attempted description of the seismic shift he had experienced started to form and be pronounced. 'I'm not exactly sure how it's all happened to tell you the truth, but I have had a guardian angel helping and guiding me through, getting away from a life that was wrong. It started at your class and so far, is working out. And well, long story short I think I've found a good place here, at least for the time being. Karen's been amazing and Joe, this wood guy, has given me work and well I'm more sorted than maybe I've ever been.' Matt stopped talking, flushed out by the effort. Then hesitant, asked, 'What's with you coming here with them? How do you know Belle? You know we knew each other… a bit,' he added. He jerked his head towards the door beyond which the women were again talking animatedly.

'Yes, she told me. I met her at a club I sometimes work. It was total love at first sight. Honestly, I know it sounds corny, but it happened just like that. She's a gem, I can't believe my luck. And Alice, well she owes you an apology, but go easy on her though she's off work with stress, I thought it would be a good idea for her to come, I hope you don't mind.'

Whether he minded or not he replied 'Sure, I've got no axe to grind, I have been pretty stressed out myself. And I'm happy for you and Belle.' Matt was relieved to hear his voice sounding genuine and more relieved to realise that he honestly wasn't disappointed, the life where he had fantasied about Belle was not his now, Karen and Joe's friendship had anchored him somewhere new. In fact, he could clearly see their compatibility. There was a halo of light around each of them that had helped launch him from a dark place. 'Congratulations to you Gus. I really am glad you found each other.'

'Me too. I didn't want it to be awkward if you were still holding a torch for her. But now please tell me what's happening with the gangsters? Are you still expecting a visit?'

'I can't explain why, but I think not,' he replied. 'Besides, I'm getting very fit with all the wood stuff so unless they come up here and catch me off guard, I feel like I could handle myself. I'm not really any threat to them so I don't think they'll bother.'

'Sure, but I want you to know I've got your back if you need help with anyone threatening you. Just give me a shout.'

Matt swallowed an overwhelming surge of grateful affection. He had never had the protection of an older brother, somebody who looked out for you when the world was big and scary or someone was giving you grief.

'And I agree,' continued Gus giving Matt a chance to recover himself, 'you are looking good. I like the new style.' And he ruffled his hair playfully.

They unwrapped the bread and cheese, pickles and crisps that Matt had fetched from the supermarket, unsure what to provide.

'Ah that's what I like to see, waiter service' said Karen with a wink to the women as the men brought a tray of food into the room. The women seemed conspiratorial. Matt was glad of the solidarity with Gus. They ate chatting pleasantly above an unspoken underworld where questions seethed like earthworms ploughing and aerating soil. Afterwards Karen declined the invitation to join them for a walk, so it was four of them who tramped outside under the yew tree and through the gate behind the cottage to go up and onto the common. 'It's slippery after the thaw,' he warned sounding like a seasoned country dweller, 'follow the fence line if I were you.'

It wasn't raining but the afternoon hung heavy with damp. Water seeped from the bare branches where droplets momentarily suspended then gave up their hold and plummeted to earth; the perfect ovoid form shattered to oblivion. The density in the atmosphere quietened all chatter as they squelched their way up to the tree line the sky low, gun metal grey. Gus and Belle walked on ahead arms playfully around each other leaving Matt and Alice walking silently behind. The wool on Alice's coat was beaded with wet, her raven dark hair shone. Sheep grazed nonchalantly as they passed, their fleeces apparently impervious.

'I….,' their voices collided talking at the same time. Both halted abruptly but Matt didn't wait long before launching again into his apology.

'Look I'm really very sorry for how I was that night. I was messed up in my mind when I said what I said to you about talking to the drug boss. It didn't come out right. I don't blame you for your reaction. I was out of order. It was stupid, I was trying to work out how they might have known where I was, and I really didn't want to mess things up for Karen she's been off the scale kind to me.'

In her turn Alice drew breath. She replied in a measured way.

'I want to apologise too; things were getting on top of me at work and I shouldn't have reacted like that. I'm sorry. But you were a bit of an idiot.'

She was relieved when Matt grinned, laughing, hands in the air. 'Yep, that's me!'

Cautiously he asked her about her work, and she surprised herself by starting to tell him all about the fucked upness of it. He knew about the care system, how it worked and didn't, from the user side of things and before they knew it, they had walked up the hill and into a descending mist, losing sight of the others completely. When a mist falls on a hillside, it drops like a blanket smothering fire. As the visual clues of the landscape disappear, direction becomes befuddled by vision shrinking, buried alive in dense air. They were suddenly disorientated. 'Let's head back' said Matt.

'What about the others?'

'Have you got a phone on you? I've almost given mine up.'.

'I do, but I doubt there will be a signal up here.'

'I reckon Gus and Belle will be able to work out how to retrace their steps. They may not have gone that far.'

Careful not to take a wrong path they turned back keeping an eye on some ghostly fence posts that loomed blearily to their right. They turned 180 degrees back on themselves.

'One false move and we could be lost for ever' said Matt cheerily

'Yes,' Alice giggled. 'I once got caught out on my own up a mountain over in North Wales when a thick fog came down. I turned around somehow and then didn't know where I was even though I had a map and a compass. Luckily a couple appeared out of the gloom they were lost too so we found our way down together.' Matt was impressed.

'That's brave to be out on your own, do you often go on adventures like that?'

'Either brave or stupid,' Alice laughed again, and he couldn't help but notice how her grey eyes were both pretty and shrewd as they crinkled at the corners when she looked happy.

She caught him gazing and for a moment their eyes locked, each slightly defiant, as if, intensified by the tunnel of soft-focus fog, they were seeing each other for the first time.

'You must have had plenty of solo adventures yourself' Alice asked, noting how without the sharply razored hair his features looked both gentler yet more rugged. And then he was explaining about having to be independent from an early age had meant becoming self-reliant, how the adventures of a looked after child were less about carefree fun and more like a battle for survival. Seeing the results of childhood deprivation manifest in the adult she walked beside left her feeling pampered and a bit uncomfortable. Matt, sensing her growing distance bounded ahead and leaping up to an overhanging branch swung like a monkey to retrieve her grin. Up ahead they could make out the diffuse silhouettes of a couple kissing.

'It seems they have found their way ok' said Matt words loaded with awkwardness and they called over to Gus and Belle who disentangled themselves. All the intimacy of the previous moments evaporated. A breeze blew, theatrically sweeping a magical cape to reveal a shard of wooded valley in the distance, treasure which then disappeared back into obscurity. The four of them headed straight back to the carpark, darkness suggesting itself at the edges of the fog. Now they came to say their goodbyes, Belle pecked him on the cheek and gave a light squeeze of his arm. Gus hugged him again and said he'd be glad if they could train together. Strange and strained after the warmth of the visit, Alice just said, thanks it was nice, and he agreed. He waved them off. His heart yearned painfully. For what exactly he wasn't sure but cut open without being stitched back together, it felt wrong that Alice should leave without them knowing when they might meet again. But she did.

There was plenty to get on with it. The quiet steady living with woods and sky, with weather and stars, with fire and cats and earth slowly warming up before the explosive thrust of spring. He and Karen acclimatised to both their mutual benefits learning the daily compromises needed to accommodate another. Joe was the fulcrum. Providing experienced tether for a young man straining against both destiny and physicality, the work with him was both demanding and relaxing and humour was the key. When either one of them hit upon frustration with an immoveable obstacle they found a way to laugh. Joe didn't mention his wife again and only once asked Matt if he had any love interest on the boil to which he replied no. After the silent crowds of snowdrops had taken their bow and the trumpeting daffodils took the stage, spring was well and truly underway. Matt started to think forwards again. As ever he simply didn't know what was in store. He was happy here, but it all felt borrowed, not fully his own life, once again he was restless.

One sharp early morning before winter was entirely banished, a message came from an unknown number asking if a visit would be ok. He responded cautiously still warily mindful that some vendettas have long memories. The reply came back instantly with apology for lack of detail. It was Alice. *Yes, to a visit. Whenever.* He was here.

And they agreed that a few mornings later they would meet on the spring equinox. Alice had spent the receding winter's weeks negotiating a minimal role with her job. She had enrolled on two courses. One on botany and the other on floristry and already had ideas about creating a small business. Without the demanding stress of daily trauma however, far from relaxed and happy, she was feeling a vast emptiness pulsing in her life. Too often she was alone, with herself as insufficient company. At these moments she started speculating about a partner and what it might mean to share. The previous month a friend had arranged a date for her. She had agreed warily. The guy was very kind. They had a pleasant evening together, respectfully skirting around each other's aloneness and he had been keen to meet her again. She however, had known from the moment she entered the restaurant that some vital ingredients were missing, that their flavours would never properly mix. He was simply too nice, over sweetened for her taste. Perhaps experience of trauma is somehow addictive in and off itself. They say the pain body wields uncommon power in order to remain intact and unthreatened by happiness. Or was it the unpredictability of the wild that Alice craved? For whenever the city tired her, into her mind came images of moor and hillside that soothed the restless weariness. This was when Matt would come into her thoughts. Before vacillating further, she had contacted him. They met again in the car park and walked without words out onto the hill. They were walking along side by side silent for a long while, sensing safety, before they began to talk. And then how they talked. As if thirsty for real conversation after weeks of drought they lapped and they guzzled, and swallowed, refreshing the dehydration of a certain kind of loneliness. It had been stored away waiting for the other, waiting to admit the other. As they neared the summit of the hill, they stopped for a drink of water by an abandoned mining works. The old walls were just the right height to sit on and swing their legs thudding against moss covered stones, children in a playground looking out over miles of field, hill, tree, and valley. The sky was wispy with high cloud and the emerald quickening of spring air held promise and potential.

Their conversation ran out, leaving them alone on the hill, their arms were touching, then their hands, then their gaze, then their lips and then a force of passion equally matched, took hold of them both. Perhaps it was the energy of the season, perhaps the long stretch of celibate solitude, who knows but these two young beings coupled with an abandon complete enough to leave them breathless and hardly able to recognise themselves. After the thrill of orgasm, they looked at each other and laughed. They were sticky and sweating, their clothes in disarray but they lay back on the slightly damp turf and laughed at the sky as if all the world was created by fucking on a hillside and that was the biggest joke. It was only the distant sight of a walker with a little dog heading their way that demanded they tidy themselves and conceal their pleasure.

The dog reached them first yapping excitedly and racing around with the fervour of recognition, the walker puffing from the climb arriving after. The little dog was licking Matt in a frenzy of excitement. Then rolling on its silky back was tickled on the tummy by Alice.

'Down, come, heel!' Shouted the man desperately, then on seeing Matt said 'ah hello it's you again, changed your mind yet about relieving me of this small monster?'

Matt mumbled something non-committal and the man continued up the hill with determined strides, calling relentlessly for the dog to follow. Alice and Matt waited until he was reasonably out of earshot then shook with laughter.

'Are you going to take on that little puppy?' She asked.

'Wasn't planning to,' he replied, 'but would you like it if I did?' They both blushed. The implication of any future was at that moment too crowded with expectation. If only they had known that billions of sperm were headed directly to an optimally fertile egg. That one of their courageous number was about to successfully permeate the egg's membrane and fertilise it. And that another lifetime was at that precise moment being calculated, a soul's calling set in motion by the same divine forces that had set the stone to make a hill upon whose flanks they had made love. But they didn't realise this yet. Instead, they walked innocently back down the hill and kissed each other goodbye, arranging that maybe next week he would visit her in her flat in the city he had left behind. But not before he would hear news of the police bungling a raid on a drugs ring who had allegedly had to change their locus of operations. They had got away with a lot but were being watched and some arrests had been made.

A baby was about to turn everything on its head as babies do, carrying within it codes and strands of other lifetimes, of a grandfather and a great grandmother resolving other lifetimes. Depending on. Who knows what. Ramifications reverberating in fractal patterns of fortune. Unfathomable connections forged by cause and effect. Consequential actions causing and effecting, defying time and rational understanding. The universe goes wheeling through the skies, breathing in and out. And humans wrestle with what goes on inside themselves, wanting it to be other than it often is, struggling when it isn't. Hanging out its washing in the light that is always there, shining, informative, gracing with brilliance and shade, the great usherette of a captivating cinema.

Acknowledgements

This story was written last year as I was forced to lay on my back when my spine fractured. I had wanted to try writing a novel and it gave me a focus while it seemed that everything else was falling apart. I have been mindful of my late mother Joan's words about another piece of writing of mine she read. 'Let's face it dear, it's not Shakespeare but I couldn't put it down.' Coming from the best-read woman I knew that was high praise and I hope it might be true for this story.

I am exceedingly grateful to have fabulous friends and family who are and have been the source of great solace, encouragement, and creative inspiration during the challenge of readjusting my capacities. I would also like to thank all the students I have been privileged to share time with and all of you who come to sit around the fire. Thank you, I deeply appreciate your presence in my life and how we are learning to be together. Most particular thanks to my wonderful co conspirator and working partner Pip Waller, my dear friend and textile queen Beck Knight who also helped design the cover of this book, the extraordinary and lovely artist, musician and creatrix of the front cover's print Sara Philpott, my beautifully creative musician son Mani Layward Wells, and last but never least my life partner, fellow seeker and firekeeper, the incomparable Michael Locke.

Printed and bound in the United Kingdom
28/01/2026
02043673-0002